*f*P

Also by Jenoyne Adams

Resurrecting Mingus: A Novel

Jenoyne Adams

Selah's Bed

a novel

Free Press
New York   London
Toronto   Sydney

FREE PRESS
A Division of Simon & Schuster, Inc.
1230 Avenue of the Americas
New York, NY 10020

First Free Press trade paperback edition 2004

Free Press and colophon are trademarks of Simon & Schuster, Inc.

For information about special discounts for bulk purchases,
please contact Simon & Schuster Special Sales:
1-800-456-6798 or business@simonandschuster.com.

Designed by Jeanette Olender
Manufactured in the United States of America

1 3 5 7 9 10 8 6 4 2

The Library of Congress has cataloged the hardcover edition as follows:
Adams, Jenoyne.
Selah's bed : a novel / Jenoyne Adams.
p. cm.
1. Married women—Fiction. 2. Grandparent and child—Fiction.
3. Terminally ill—Fiction.   I. Title.
PS3551.D3745 S4 2003
813'.6   dc21   2002040893
ISBN 978-0-671-78784-4

*This book
is for everyone who has
gotten back up.*

It is not a garment I cast off this day,
But a skin that I tear with my own hands.

Kahlil Gibran

Selah's Bed

Chapter One

Sex was a way to stop the crying, the powerlessness of not feeling beautiful. She always felt beautiful under lustful hands. Lustful hands can't lie. The want, greed, and emptiness is real. That type of emptiness can't be imagined. And she trusted it because she understood it. The magic that disillusioned others about loving was what she liked most—the emptiness always comes back. She could count on that. And as long as it did, she could keep believing that she didn't need promises of forever.

Selah knew that real love only costs twenty-five cents. That's what she charged the neighborhood boys in Waterman Gardens where she grew up. Waterman Gardens was more than a project; it was the entire world. Starting just below Bradley Elementary School and ending just before Kmart, between Baseline and Tippecanoe, everything she needed was within three blocks of its pink concrete walls. She and Tina Perkins used to sit on the great wall of their city, their ten-year-old Vaseline-slicked legs crossed and dangling as boys with little

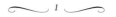

afros and grown-up appetites passed. Selah noticed way back then that boys weren't so different than men. She watched little boys play basketball; she watched grown men play basketball. They all liked dogs, remote control cars, and women.

Selah studied her neighborhood. She recognized that chase was an early form of sex and that the possibility of ending up with a man that visited late nights and never took out the trash was real. She was intimate with women she'd one day become. Not intimate in a sad way, but in the concrete way of staring at your mother and under-standing what you'll look like at sixty-five. But Selah would not look like her mother; she decided that the day she took home her first training bra from JCPenney's with her grandmother. Selah would look like Mama Gene and all the other grandmas, aunties, and moth-ers in her neighborhood who had the courage not to leave.

Staying could be difficult between these walls. Waterman Gar-dens was a low-rent mecca for black women. The kind of place you agree to until you can find something better and end up collecting your social security in. The units were joined in twos with a slab of gray concrete on either side for parking. Behind the parking spaces were two parallel brick walls with clothesline cord strung between them. Every back door opened to a sprawling common area of green grass and trees used for shade, climbing, and switches. Front doors opened to wide streets with exotic names that intersected each - other's curves. This wasn't a woman's paradise, it was more of a per-manent holding tank. The kind of place you could move sideways in, but never up and out of. A mother was lucky to get a two-story apartment. Most families squeezed all its members into one or two rooms and hoped their name would rise to the top of the waiting list for a three or four bedroom vacancy. Selah didn't understand until she was older why her neighborhood was considered a ghetto. *Ghetto* was a term that showed the low expectation wider society had for her underprivileged world. And at the same moment this occurred to her, she also realized that her sprawling neighborhood would have been called *condos* if white yuppies lived within its walls.

At ten, Selah's world was already complicated by the responsibility of knowing. Pink birthday tights and silk ribboned ponytails were only symptoms of childhood. Red lipstick was already on the inside of her. Selah admired the five and seven year olds who still found completion in colored supermarket balls and swing sets. Despite their fifth-grade status, she and all of her girlfriends were women. Their teachers knew it, so did their older brothers' friends. It was their mothers who were the last to find out. The girls hid their womanhood from their mothers in school bathrooms and sleepovers, in missing underwear and booty-shaking playground cheers:

My name is Selah . . . Yeah,
and I am fine . . . Yeah,
if you don't like it . . . Yeah,
kiss my behind.
Roll Call Sha-boogie, check, check me out.

These girls hid their womanhood, but more than anywhere, they hid it in summer days on the "Gate," their legs dangling against pink concrete, their mouths sucking on orange Popsicle sticks, and their minds filled with loving.

Out of Tina, Tasha-Marie, and Carla, Selah was the least talkative of her crew. She thought it was because she was the biggest sinner of all of them. In Selah's mind, the biggest sinner needed to know when to keep her mouth shut. Maybe if she'd gone to church more, - she'd have felt forgiven for her sins. Even the most heathen children had to go to church in summer. No weekend homework, no excuses. The church van never came for Selah. And she connected this absence with her uncontrollable urge to do things she wasn't supposed to. To Sunday summers of amazon grass and yellow short-shorts. To her missing mother and father. To a God that never answered when she asked. And to boys with quarters who would pay to touch budding breasts behind backyard trash cans.

Chapter Two

It was easier for Selah to find nakedness in men. That's why she photographed them. Even as a photojournalist for the *Sentinel* and mainstream newspapers, she always tried to find the man behind the story. She did this because women often came with their pretensions first. It wasn't Selah's bag to have to pick and rummage through their surfaces to find the truth—this wasn't the case with most men. As soon as their clothing dropped, their bravado dropped as well. They wanted to be seen, particularly by a woman. They needed a space to be vulnerable; Selah was this space. That's why men opened to her, unpolished and pomegranate red before her camera.

Selah thought at times that this transparency was a sort of apology—a way to show the women throughout their lives that they were sorry. Sometimes it was a mother being apologized to, sometimes the ex-girlfriend or the mother of their fifth child. Selah saw their collective need for forgiveness. It especially showed up in the penis. How it would coil itself into a pungent knot, hide behind a thick thigh,

Jenoyne Adams

or sometimes, how it would betray its owner by hardening in front of the camera. Selah always felt sorry for a man when this happened. She understood how the penis could act in direct opposition to the eyes. Her body and emotions were often in this type of conflict— the way her hurt would drive her to want men besides Parker. The aching would start in the lining of her vagina, like the warning signs of an approaching period. Selah obeyed the ache. She obeyed anytime her body responded viscerally to anything. She had stopped crying years ago. Nothing could hurt her to tears anymore—not the death of her grandfather or Mama Gene's delusions because of the pills. Selah wanted something to jolt her. Maybe she would be whole again. Maybe she would feel somewhere other than between her legs.

"It's natural," she would tell the man. "I can see you feeling something real right now. It's in your eyes. Trust this, your penis will come around."

Eventually it would and Selah would gain such joy from the revelation. She rejoiced for anyone who could turn her words into action. She'd been trying to do that in her own life for a long time.

Selah worked out of two studios. One studio was primarily a gallery and the other was where she shot and housed her photography equipment. Umbra Gallery was located on Degnan Boulevard across the street from the World Stage Performance Gallery and three storefronts down. Because she often photographed neighborhood men nude or sparsely clothed, she never exhibited works on the main boulevard of small restaurants, jazz spots, and ethnic galleries. Her front display windows were smoked black with a small sign in the corner that read ENTRANCE IN REAR. Her clientele consisted mostly of women in their thirties and forties, repeat customers who added pieces to their repertoires with the unveiling of each new collection. One of her most popular collections was one on neighborhood drummers.

Because Selah had an affinity toward Afro-Cuban jazz and African rhythms, she had primarily asked drummers from these traditions to participate. The sittings took place over a period of four months and each shoot lasted two to three hours. It takes time to shoot quality photographs, Selah believed, especially nudes. This was because people are used to dressing up for photographs. Putting on our best suits and fullest makeup—earrings, matching socks, clean underwear, perfume. Selah maintained that photography could be the grandest illusion of how we wished things were. A photograph can conceal last night's fights and familial resentments. We can be beautiful, thin, and seamlessly perfect on these waxed pages.

Selah's goal was to capture the opposite of this. She wanted the curved spine and freckles mid-chest. She wanted the wet eyes and uneven smile. And because she knew that the nude human body could be as plain as a block of unformed wood, she took painstaking care to treat her subjects with the utmost respect.

The drummers would come in one by one and Selah would shoot them against a black velvet backdrop, draped floor to ceiling. She would sit on the blond wood floor of the small studio with her camera hanging against her stomach from its black strap. Between sips of lavender tea, she'd ask the men questions about how they started playing, how they felt about their hands, and why their favorite drum was their favorite. Selah would ask them to undress slowly, as they felt compelled to. "Let what you know to be true about yourself guide you," she'd say.

Selah loved it whenever she saw sweat bead around a hairline. The natural perspiration increased the animal magnetism of her work and proved that her studio environment was working. She kept the windows shut with a small freestanding fan circulating slowly in the corner opposite the door. The only furniture in the room was a liquor cabinet and a wooden bar stool that clients often sat on until they relaxed into the vibe of the shoot. The shades were drawn and lavender mixed with frankincense burned sweet in the stairway that joined the lower studio to the upstairs room. Selah sweated a lot during these sessions and dressed in layers, so often she and her subjects peeled off clothing at the same time.

Sometimes the drummers would ask her questions as well.

"Do you ever get turned on photographing men this way?"

"Yes."

"Do you ever act on it?"

"Never during a shoot."

"Have you ever wanted to?"

"Yes."

"How do you control yourself?"

"It's the only time I control myself."

She was always honest with the men. A nude man not engaged in a sexual act had more radar than the most scantily clothed woman, any day. Selah needed a man to feel safe with her in order for the shoot to work so she held herself to the same pact of honesty she held them to: "Always be honest with me. If I ask you a question you don't want to answer or if there is a position you don't feel comfortable with, let me know."

"Are you attracted to me?"

"I think you're beautiful."

"Do you want me?"

"Yes, but I won't have you." She'd smile.

A man would laugh after asking her that, partly at her answer and partly at himself for asking. Selah would snap this shot, the camera's frame hiding the laughter in her eyes, a serious expression set on her lips and chin.

Something in her lit up when a man flirted with her like this. There was an innocence to the proposition in the question. The woman in her wanted to believe it was the power of her female magnetism and not the vulnerability of them trusting her. It was possible that after a man was clothed again he wouldn't even be attracted to her pliable thighs and brown breasts with darker brown nipples that he could get lost in for days. Selah knew this and for that and other reasons she kept her shoots absolutely professional. She didn't want to violate the men; she knew the difficulty of sharing nudity with a stranger. And while the man put back on his clothes, Selah would take the film out of her camera and place it in the upstairs safe inside her developing closet.

Any attempt at a secondary sexual advance was useless. Selah had never had sex with a client before at this point in her life. The one time she did, she fell in love. Not with him, but with the possibility his presence left behind. This was real love, the kind she had for Parker, but never allowed herself to feel. The kind she tried to sex away with strangers. This man was a traveling moment that made it possible for her to be still.

Aside from clients, Selah never had intercourse with married men either. Considering she was married, she was never fully sure why she held this conviction. She'd determined a married man couldn't possibly sex her right. He would always be split between *her* and, as Mama Gene would put it, "the *poot nan* he should be tending to in the first place." Selah had enough conflict of her own already. She needed potency, a man who could pound into her and be free of subconsciousness. *Subconsciousness,* Selah maintained, was a disease that scars people worse than the most terrible of conscious thoughts.

Subconsciousness could drive a person crazy if they suppressed themselves long enough. Selah had already done this to herself before and come back; she didn't want to scar anyone else.

Once he was nude, Selah would have the man play his drums. - She'd squat low to the ground to photograph the way the drummer's thighs braced the drum's wooded frame and pulsed hard in response to rhythms created when his hands struck the cream colored animal skin. They would lose themselves: Selah in her photography, the man in his music. Her favorite piece in the series was a mixed medium collage where she combined the shots of five drummers with red and bronze tempera lines overlapping the jagged edges of the torn sepia-toned photographs. Each man had an intensity in his face all his own, which Selah recalled vividly every time she looked at the framed 20 x 25 original in the comfort of her upper room.

Chapter Three

Grandma Gene used to say things she meant, but really didn't. More to Papa Frank than to Selah. The kind of things that make you lean back in the couch and focus on the television buzz that no one else hears. The kind of things that would stop Papa Frank from taking out the trash or telling her he loved her. Some nights when Mama Gene had told Papa Frank way more than he needed to know that she thought about him in one sitting, it would be three o'clock in the afternoon on the next day before he would acknowledge her. He'd get out of bed at 4:00 A.M., and instead of going down to San Bernardino High School where he had been a janitor for the past fifteen years, he'd grab his pole from the four-inch space between the refrigerator and the wall, take his tackle box from under the sink, and head down to Fifth Street Park to catch bluegill and the occasional catfish with the raw chicken livers he stole from Mama Gene's icebox.

When Papa Frank returned home around twelve that afternoon

with four or five fish on his chain, only then would Mama Gene know he had skipped work. Mama Gene would then need to call Mr. Michaels the head custodian to let him know that Frank Mathis was under the weather and might be out for another day or so. It was entirely up to Mama Gene how many days Papa would miss. Everything depended on Mama Gene's mouth and how well she was able to tack it shut and let him forget a little. Papa Frank never called in for himself when he missed work. He figured that was Mama Gene's job because it was always her fault when he missed and Papa Frank could miss a whole week if he damned well pleased and Mama Gene made him mad enough.

Papa would find himself a nice spot under the shade tree in the common area backyard, place Mama Gene's cutting board on two shunts of wood, and commence to scale and cut up the fish. Papa Frank could sit out there for hours under leaves that never swayed for lack of breeze. San Bernardino did this every year before the beginning of summer, sucked its breath back into the fault lines of its desert skin to let residents swelter in dry, sun-baked heat. But that - didn't matter to Papa Frank. He was a native of Bullhead City, Arizona, and San Bernardino could never brand him the way *The Bull* had. Besides, Papa knew how to imagine himself a breeze. A tricky one, that made him press his Stingy Brim down tight over his ears so his hat wouldn't fly away in the wind.

Mama Gene usually started dinner early on these days. Cut up potatoes and put mushroom and cheese grits on the stove, all the while complaining under her breath about how Papa Frank's funky fish was disturbing the quality of her own imaginary breeze.

"And you bett'r not bring them fish heads in the house when - you're done neither," she'd scream from the stove, her voice traveling upstream through the screen door net, toward the backyard. "Put them heads in a bag before you put 'em in the trash tin."

Selah's Bed

Mama Gene didn't have to look through the kitchen window to know that Papa Frank wasn't paying her a damned bit of attention.

"You can ignore me all you want to, Mathis, but see what happens if your bony-shouldered behind brings those heads up in here."

Mama Gene wasn't a nagger, she was a positioner. A person who waited until the right moment to drop crystallized hurt on you. That's why Papa Frank would stop talking to her in the first place. Once she told Papa that his mother never really liked his kettle-black ass much no way and there wasn't any use in him crying over her death and carrying on like he was. The truth was that his mother *didn't* like him and Mama Gene hated her for it, but she never revealed that part to Mathis.

By the time she was old enough to tie her own shoes, Selah worried that Mama Gene would say something like that to her about her own mother. It never happened; Selah realized over time that it wouldn't. Maybe the real truth was that though Papa Frank and his mother didn't get along, his momma really did love him. And maybe, somewhere inside her, Mama Gene wasn't sure that Selah's mother did.

Ruthie was Mama Gene's only daughter. Mama Gene had raised her by herself until she met Papa Frank when Ruthie was five. Frank's mother, Francis, rented Mama Gene the converted garage in exchange for day work around the big house and one-third of the electric bill.

The garage was cozy but small. Every time Mama Gene bought or was given a new piece of furniture, she threw an old piece away so not to feel cluttered. The only thing the garage didn't have was a running toilet and bath. Mama Gene kept an enamel pot under the sink for midnight emergencies and used the bathroom in the big house where Frank and his mother lived for bathing and number-two business.

Francis Mathis liked Ruthie Mae and didn't mind having a female child following her around while Mama Gene completed her day work of scrubbing pots and windows. Mrs. Mathis even volunteered to tend to Ruthie Mae at night when Mama Gene went to her real job. But widow Mathis didn't end up watching Ruthie half as much as Frank did. Since Mama Gene worked nights from 7:00 P.M. to 4:00 A.M. and Frank's mother was taken to going to bed early, Ruthie ended up entertaining Frank for the better portion of the evening in the small garage. Besides, Mama Gene and Frank had grown fond of each other over a period of months and had come to consider themselves a couple. Not the type that would marry, but the type that enjoyed each other's company for what it was and shared bills every so often.

When Frank baby-sat Ruthie, he would sit back in the shit brown loveseat, pull the coffee table to his knees, adjust the table's slant by tightening the front leg screw into the worn particle board, then center the table-top radio between his legs. Ruthie would immediately start in. As Papa Frank drank his after-work beer, Ruthie would Shuffle the Truck, sliding her feet across the green squares in the linoleum. Next she'd try jump rope tricks or sing "Jingle Bells" into the sticky summer heat of the small room. Frank would open his eyes every so often and smile, "That's nice Ruthie," then close his eyes again and throw his mind back into his radio show. Each of Papa Frank's halfhearted attempts to appease Ruthie's need for complete attention would draw her closer to him. She'd smile big, giggle fake laughter into his face, tickle him, ride his leg like a pony, and Monday night of *The Fat Man* radio show would fall to the wayside until her appetite for attention tuckered her to sleep.

When Mama Gene got back from the convalescent hospital twenty minutes after four to the wasted electricity of radio snow and Ruthie's long, five-year-old legs sprawled across a sleeping Papa Frank, Mama Gene would snatch the old leather belt from Papa - Frank's pants hanging on the back of the bathroom door and beat - Ruthie's fresh behind.

"What-have-I-told-your-little-ass-'bout-climbing-on-grown-men's-laps?" Each drop of the belt punctuated Mama Gene's words. She'd grab one of Ruthie's skinny, flailing arms and spank her over to the twin bed in the corner of the room. "Mat-his-is-not-your-dad-dy. Let-me-see-you-do-this-a-gain-and-see-what-hap-pens-to-your-string-bean-behind."

Papa Frank would sit still on the couch not saying a word until Mama Gene calmed down. She'd snatch the radio cord out of the wall socket and head toward the bathroom to place Papa Frank's belt back on his pants.

"Dry it up, Ruthelen Mae," she'd yell, taking her seat next to Papa Frank. "And Mathis, you know your momma charges me for every last bit of that electricity, so why are you wasting my money? The - radio's been signed off for hours."

Papa Frank would nod, knowing there wasn't any usefulness in trying to talk her down. There wasn't any use in her spanking the daylights out of Ruthie Mae or telling Papa Frank about the radio staying on too long. Ruthie would always be attracted to the laps of men and the radio snow would be replaced by white television snow from a round-screen twelve-inch television set that would sit be-tween Papa Frank's sleeping legs many a night before Mama Gene could afford herself an apartment in Waterman Gardens.

Sometimes Selah wondered why Mama Gene never talked about Ruthie much. Anytime Ruthie chanced upon Selah's grandmother's home, Mama Gene lit up like a neon open-for-business sign and cooked like dignitaries were visiting. Ruthie would play daughter and loving mommy for a few days, but this wasn't her nature. She'd birthed Selah two days before she turned sixteen and abandoned her before her afterbirth menstrual cycle became regular again. Ruthie had talked a lot about giving Selah up during her first month of motherhood, but that was just crap because there wasn't any such thing as black baby adoption. The only people who wanted a black child were its parents. If the parents were nincompoops, that left relatives or the state until the streets were an option. Mama Gene treated Selah like her second daughter, even before Ruthie moved permanently out of the room that Selah would spend most of her childhood and young adulthood in.

Ruthie Mae removed herself from Mama Gene's house gradually. The last things to go were Jackie Wilson's smile and the 8 x 10 photograph of the Dells in powder blue duster jackets that hung above Selah's white bassinet. Mama Gene knew what Ruthie was doing, but didn't stop her. She noticed Ruthie Mae's lightening laundry load. Noticed that Ruthie never left the house without a bag under her arm or an extra sweater wrapped around her waist. She wanted to disappear piece by piece until Selah was the only proof she had ever been there.

Mama Gene could never find it in herself to be as hard on Ruthie Mae as she was on men. She understood women. She understood the sacrifices most women made every day just to comb their children's hair and clean their behinds. Every time a mother smiled at one of her children or rubbed Johnson's baby powder on a newborn chest, Mama Gene knew what this was worth. And whereas men began to grasp the universal moan most fully in times of death, most women inherited it with childbirth.

Ruthie Mae wanted to skirt this pain in her life. She would party herself straight to Beelzebub if she had to, but she would not waste her chocolate thighs bouncing a baby to bed every night in a small pea-colored room in her mother's two-bedroom ghetto apartment. She would not work for minimum wage and cheat the welfare department only to have to borrow back three of the five dollars she loaned a girlfriend earlier in the week. She would not sacrifice herself for Selah; she just wouldn't.

Mama Gene did not blame Ruthie Mae; she was familiar with the exchanges a woman made to consider herself a good mother. Ruthie Mae had gotten out while she could, before guilt and responsibility had swallowed the resistance in her spine. Ruthie Mae had done what Eugenia Wells, a tall, brown skinned, seventeen-year-old curve of a girl with no husband, didn't have the courage to do. Eugenia didn't have someone to make sacrifices for her child that she wasn't willing to make herself. So when Ruthie Mae handed Selah to Mama Gene when Selah cried, or when she was hungry, or when her diaper needed changing, Mama Gene took Selah from Ruthie Mae knowing that everything that needed to be said, had been said in the changing of arms.

Ruthie wanted all the accoutrements that long legs, a big booty, and tight hips could give a young woman. The not-so-young man Ruthie got knocked up by was what Mama Gene called a "jive ass - momma's nigga." The kind that would suck his momma's teat dry until he found another titty to latch on to.

Mama Gene had always told Ruthie Mae that it was better to share her bed with a one-legged dog than with a sorry piece of man with good looks and a high sperm count. She didn't listen; she was in love. And he loved her back . . . Ruthie Mae and both of his other sixteen-year-old girlfriends who lay on their backs to establish him as a real pimp.

When Ruthie did visit, Selah knew who she was. Selah called Grandma Gene, Momma, and Ruthie Mae, sister. This would piss Ruthie off and she'd pick fights with Mama Gene and tell her she was going to pack Selah up and take her with her when she left.

"Well hurry up," Mama Gene would say. "That way I don't have to pay Frieda Perkins's oldest daughter five dollars to watch her tonight."

That would always be the end of Ruthie's visit and the end of Selah being played with like a baby doll and tossed aside until Ruthie felt like playing house again in a few months or longer than that. But even then, Selah enjoyed the one-day potty training sessions and putting lotion in Ruthie's hair to smooth it out with the wrong side of the brush. Ruthie would huff out of the house and tell Mama Gene she'd be back for Selah in a few hours, then she'd slip off again like music on the radio. Your favorite song never lasts forever. And had Selah been old enough to have a favorite song, she may have understood her relationship with her mother. She was just a baby. All Selah wanted was to pull her small fingers through her mother's Jergens scented hair and have Ruthie Mae be there when she woke up.

Chapter Four

There are places words can't get to. Where specificity pintucks itself behind a feeling the tongue can't wrap around. She would feel them coming. The over-bubblings of regret that constricted the throat and made her long for the remedy of death. There are early graves set aside for people who need them. But Selah was not ready for death because God was not ready for her.

She would have to live through her birthings. Harness them within the trappings of flesh and somehow manage to survive the pain of - memory's return. The cost was a piece of sanity. A small piece of color, barely discernible in the kaleidoscope of being. She'd been here many times before. And when she was able to stand up again, she would leave this space inside herself. Cover it over like a wound and pretend to be whole again.

"Hush up," Selah said, closing the back of her camera. She placed the shot roll of film into the black pouch attached to her belt then commenced to reload.

"I promise," he said. "You'll want to keep me on your nightstand like incense and a thick blunt."

The surety of his tone let her know that being nude for him was like having on his best suit.

"I don't smoke," Selah said. "And I like my men the way I like my camera. Old. Keep painting." She bent slightly at the knee while adjusting the lens of her Minolta SRT 100 with her right hand.

"Tell me this," he turned away from the canvas streaked with circular strokes of layered purples and browns, a cranberry colored knot emerging from the painting's center, "don't this look like something you can work with?"

Reenie looked down, the brush held high in his hand like he was taking an oath. The dead weight of his penis posed soundly against his leg.

"Don't show me nothing you don't want blown up forty by sixty."

"If you can handle it, I can make it happen," his eyes smiled mischievously, then slipped behind the curtain of his reddish-brown locks. Reenie turned toward the canvas, slowly, giving Selah full view of his periphery before continuing to paint.

He should be ashamed of himself, she thought. He was too young for Selah and he knew it. She smiled. He wanted her anyway. The sweet pungency of his scent floating above the lavender oil burning in the stairway told her so. Reenie had made his intentions known. Something in him longed for a seasoned woman. Selah didn't blame him— a slow-cooked pot roast of a woman was better than a microwaved and processed deli slice any day.

Selah didn't want him the way a woman craves a lover though. He was like fresh dirt after rain. She liked the way the newness of his manhood smelled. *The smell is the first thing to go,* she thought. The best cologne could never hide the souring effects of compromise on an older man's skin. The more she clicked, the sadder Selah became.

She remembered how this process of being broken down had happened to her. She should have warned him against fading. Told him to wear sunscreen on his soul. But she'd had young lovers before and she knew. Admonitions work best on those who have already been broken.

"I think I have all the shots I need," she reattached the lens cover and let the camera dangle against her stomach. "Thank you and I'll send you a signed and numbered poster of the one I choose for the series."

She didn't mean to turn cold. She didn't mean to suck the rays out of her smile and leave him to wonder how a shell of a woman had convinced him to pose nude for her camera. But she had to. She had to save herself from the regret creeping over her body like nightfall. He would have to learn heaviness somewhere else.

The sweat-aches started in her chest. Selah climbed the sixteen narrow steps to the upper room holding both sides of the wall in the stairwell to brace herself. She didn't blow out the lavender as she normally did or bring the four rolls of film up from the studio and lock them in the closet safe. What was important was the ache. The finger of God burning a hole of memory in her chest.

She could make it go away if she would just write. A few lines, something to make her world make sense. This was the only thing that helped when she got like this. She didn't expect anyone to understand; she didn't understand. All she knew was that the loss would overtake her if she didn't overtake it first.

I write you to make things different.

Selah tried to remember how the letter went.

I try to make myself something other than I really am.

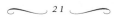

She lay on her side in the unmade bed, scribbling barely discernible words on the backside of a proof sheet. She had paper; she had reams and reams of paper, varying in texture and thickness. That didn't matter. She just needed to put the words somewhere.

Selah dug the tip of the pen into the proof's waxy surface. The paper gave against the softness of the bed.

I am a nineteen-year-old mother.

For years, she had written pieces of this letter over and over again. On napkins, the spine of her Bible she rarely opened. There were many letters. The originals were written on letterhead with sunflowers at the top center. She stored them in a box under the bed. A plain box. Brown corrugated board. The letters were creased twice so that the body and the two ends were the same length. They did not smell like anything and time had not faded the ink. Each letter had its own envelope from Selah Wells addressed to nowhere. Where do you send letters to a child that God took away too soon?

Selah would try to find peace in this space. She would write and reread these letters over and over and over again because the hardest question is this: Who consoles the mother who is left behind?

Chapter Five

Selah and Tina beat Luwanda Lewis's albino ass after school that day for telling the truth like a bold-faced, hurtful lie. The situation started because Tina and Selah had decided ten minutes into a twenty-minute recess that they wanted to play tetherball and Luwanda's court was the easiest one to take over.

"Loser's out," Selah said, jumping into the court. She tapped the pole twice, then stepped to the south side of the white line signifying that she'd chosen her side of the court. She always chose the south side at last recess—that way the sun wouldn't be in her eyes as she played.

Luwanda grabbed the dingy white rope attached to the ball and flung hard. The chain at the top of the pole clanked and the ball spun wildly. Selah ducked then stopped the ball.

Luwanda squinted in Selah's direction, but avoided her eyes.

"I already tapped in permanent," Luwanda said with attitude, trying to yank the ball from Selah's hand by the rope.

"Didn't nobody hear you," Tina said, standing with her legs agape from behind the imaginary waiting line.

Selah socked the ball with the side of her fist a few times and the ball spun smooth and quick around the pole.

"Y'all just trying to take my court."

"Can't nobody take your court if you win. Right Tina?"

"Right on," Tina answered back.

"I was here first. I'ma tell Mrs. Davis."

"You ain't gonna tell nobody." Selah stopped the ball again and placed the rope under her arm while she loosened the wedgy from her shorts. "You ready or what, 'cause if you need to think about it, I'll just play Tina 'til you decide."

"You can't just come and change my rules."

"Already did, come on Tina, she ain't really trying to play. She just likes the sound of her own voice."

Tina jumped into the court and the two of them played a game of keep away, Selah throwing the ball over Luwanda's head and Tina hitting it too hard for Luwanda to catch.

"Just sit down, Luwanda," Tina said, slamming the ball with her cupped palm.

"Yeah, Luwanda, go play with the five year olds."

They laughed. Luwanda's skin grew pink in anger as Selah and Tina settled into a real game. They ignored her. They talked over and around her like she didn't exist. Luwanda stormed off of the court. Recess was almost over and their coup was almost solidified when Luwanda yelled from the dodge ball circle halfway across the playground, "Selah Wells, that's why yo momma's uhh HO on Mount Vernon."

Tina and Selah didn't even look at each other. They took off running after Luwanda so hard Selah's side started to ache. They would catch her, but it wouldn't be until after school. After they waited for her on the backside of the school because they knew she'd try to take the long way home. Luwanda Daelin Lewis would never think of saying a thing like that again about anybody's momma and Selah would never forget how she and Tina beat the purple beads out of her head and gladly got suspended for one week for doing it.

Chapter Six

Every so often Selah felt the need to cut the matting herself. She took the X-Acto matting knife from its box and sat it next to the 25 x 50 piece of plywood she had laid on the floor. Selah liked to mat special pieces herself and she always did them in the upper room of her studio.

Some people needed special tables and rulers to mat a photograph properly. All Selah needed was a sharp blade, a good grip, and an oldie but goodie tune floating around in her head. She placed the purple board in the center of the plywood and began to cut. The trick was to stay calm and not let the oddly angled blade go too deep. Selah sat on her knees facing the only window in the match-box-size room. The white wooded cross separating the four distinct squares of glass showcased the light as the sun filtered its rays into the room. She sang.

"Rock the boat, don't rock the boat baby. Rock the boat, don't tip the boat over."

Selah's Bed

The grandness of her faded denim–covered behind swayed to the music. Once done with all four cuts, she paused to get into a few tight hits to the left of the *Bump.* She placed the brown piece of matting on the wood.

Sometimes Selah felt that she could reach back through her entire life through song. And she could. "Rock the Boat" always reminded her of the seventies, which reminded her of the *Bump,* which reminded her of Parker and how they used to make love under the bleachers.

Parker used to like the way Selah smelled. Baby powder and cherry lip gloss, mixed with Mama Gene's White Shoulders perfume on her brown wrist. That's what attracted her to him. He said that she was the cornucopia of womanhood. Whatever cornucopia was, Selah knew it was good though she didn't look up the word until months after Michelle.

After running into each other every Monday, Wednesday, and Friday mornings accidentally-on-purpose and coincidentally hanging out after track practice once or twice a week, Selah and Parker's language changed from "Maybe I'll see you tomorrow" to "I'll meet you by four thirty." Selah liked this change. She didn't need Tasha-Marie and Carla with her anymore to cover up the seriousness of her intentions. She was there to see Parker—because he wanted her to be.

Selah liked the way they climbed under the bleachers and sat on their jackets in the dirt under the wood and metal structure into the early evening. Parker liked to lean on his left elbow and adjust his body lower than Selah's, the side of his face resting between her breast and underarm as she sat upright with her ankles crossed. Selah used to be concerned about this. Concerned that maybe Secret deodorant just wasn't strong enough and a good whiff of her all day funk would knock her out of his affections. Parker thought her musk was sweet, though. He said it made him want to be up under her.

Selah would laugh because every time he said that it made her feel more comfortable with herself.

"Okay, keep telling me that and I'm gonna stop wearing deodorant, period."

"You know that's what I want you to do, girl; I'd even lick that Massengil freshness from between your—you know."

He lowered his face toward her crotch.

"Get off of me," she pushed him up by his face. "You just want me to smell like you do after you finish running up and down that rubber track."

Parker smiled and kissed the outside of her pink-and-blue-striped blouse.

"Is that so bad baby . . . that I want you to smell like me?" He kissed her again.

He was changing. His voice got thick when he wanted to touch her.

"No . . . I can't say that . . . it's a bad thing," she stumbled over her words as he put his free hand on the outside of her right breast and squeezed it in a way that would have hurt had it not been his hand that was doing it.

"You got to believe in somethin', why not believe in me," he closed his eyes. *"How could you treat your man so mean and cruel . . ."*

Parker moved this time with surety when he placed his face in her crotch. He lifted his head. *"Something I got to say,"* he mumbled into the polyester between her legs. *"When you left, you took all my love away-ay."*

"That's not what he says, Parker," she spoke low.

"To the land of funk—funk." He lifted his head and smiled.

Parker did this all the time, changed the words to songs and mixed different songs together. He made her laugh and sink deeper into her want for him. And they would take turns taking mouthfuls of each other until their tongues were rough and their lips hurt.

Chapter Seven

Selah sat between Mama Gene and Papa Frank on the long front seat of Papa Frank's truck, her right arm sweating under the weight of her grandmother's loose flesh. Selah gave herself until the third red light to ask the question, then until the sixth green one. She angled her face up toward her grandmother's.

"Why that ugly girl call Ruthie Mae a *ho?*"

Selah felt Mama Gene's arm jump. She knew she was getting a whoppin'. One, for asking the question and two, for beating up Luwanda. But all Mama Gene said as she looked straight ahead, her pocketbook held on her lap with both hands, was that Selah shoulda beat color into the pink ridges of the little girl's ears and only then should she have stopped.

"Don't you ever let nobody talk about your momma like she ain't worth the smell of their spit. Even if you hear a grown person doin' it, tell 'um your grandmomma got something for them. Your momma's just a free spirit and my heart ain't got room enough to hold her; Lord knows I've tried."

• • •

That week off from school, Selah and Tina became the queens of the neighborhood playground. They stole pomegranates from the corner yard on Elm Street and peeled them with dirt-caked fingernails. The next time Selah saw Ruthie Mae, she was eight years old with a musk smell developing under her arms. She noticed it after pushing Tina Perkins on the swing. As Tina pumped strong with her legs, Selah pushed hard and fast thinking that if she pushed hard enough, Tina would do a full rotation over the bar and never even fall off. After they were worn out, the two of them sat with shoulders touching on the concrete border of the sandbox.

"You stink like skunk," Tina said, frowning her face.

"Nuh uh, that's you," Selah said back, scooting two butt-widths away.

"Bet you a quarter it's you," Tina retorted.

"A dime it's not."

"Okay, a dime and you have to give Jerome a Valentine's Day card that says 'I love you.' "

"Jerome who?" Selah said, laughing and covering her mouth with her dusty, red stained hands.

"Jerome Jenkins, the boy in our class that you stare at like you like him."

"Uggh, I don't stare at no stupid boy. That boy got jacked-up teeth. I don't want no boyfriend with crooked butter yellow teeth no way." Selah thought for a second. "Well if you lose, you have to give an 'I love you' card to Keif Henderson." Selah threw herself off of the sandbox border onto the grass in laughter.

"You nasty, Selah; that boy got cooties and wears high-waters all the time."

Selah jumped up to give herself a running start. Tina started to follow behind her though Selah hadn't said anything chase-worthy yet.

"Tina and Keif, sittin' in a tree . . ."

"I'm gonna kick your butt," Tina started to run.

Selah ran faster, and all the while she kept her arms wrapped around her shoulders, pretending she was Tina kissing Keith.

When Tina caught up to her, she grabbed the waistband of -

Selah's shorts, pulled her to the ground, and put her face in Selah's armpit.

"See, I told you it was you. Take it back about Keif."

Selah shook her head no.

"Take it back or I'll tell Jerome you want to have his kids."

"Okay then, I take it back."

As Selah and Tina split ways, Selah placed her hand into her armpit and then to her nose. It was her. It was a bitter smell mixed with sweat and grass. Selah liked it. For weeks she would put her hands into her armpit area to make sure that her special smell was still there. And five months later she would give Tina the dime and Jerome the Valentine's Day card with *I love you* on it, only she didn't sign it.

The streetlights popped on when Selah was twenty steps from the back door. Selah made her way directly to the kitchen. Ruthie Mae and Mama Gene were standing at the stove. Ruthie was stirring a can of stewed tomatoes into the okra; Mama Gene was observing.

Selah had to hide her smile; seeing her mother was better than when Mama Gene made blueberry pancakes for breakfast and didn't make Selah take any cod liver oil.

"Hi, Mama Gene. Hi, Ruthie—I mean, Momma."

"Take your hand off of my wall. I've done told you about that, Selah. Go wash your dirty hands and spray some of my Secret deodorant under your little arms; you smell like you've been wrestling an orangutan."

Mama Gene was happy, Selah could tell. She had taken most of the food from the refrigerator to narrow down what she would cook for Ruthie Mae. Still, happy as she was, that was no reason to embarrass Selah by screaming at her, albeit softer than normal, in front of company.

Chapter Eight

Neither Parker Sr. nor Glodine would have ever thought that white flight would turn their thriving one-love neighborhood from almost suburban to lite-ghettoesque in less than twelve years. Parker Marvelle Lareaux Jr. grew up on Home Street between Muscott Boulevard and Magnolia. His parents bought their house in the early sixties when the neighborhood was becoming largely *mixed* and black folks were seemingly welcomed. Their four bedroom, two bathroom house was situated mid-block and the backyard gate gave Parker and his younger brother Stewart immediate access to the baseball diamond at the edge of the school yard. Though Parker Sr. and Glodine said they didn't mind the *coloring* of surrounding blocks, they constantly checked their neighbors' lawns for curb appeal and notified them immediately if trash was overflowing or their pet *went* in Glodine's miniature shrub roses.

Parker Jr. was aware of what the neighborhood called his parents. The names stuck so that new neighbors were quickly acclimated to the who's who of the mid-block kingdom. And though Parker Jr.

vowed to never call his mother "Thunder Thighs Chartreuse," because of his own heart-shaped thighs and yellow skin, "Daddy Shit Bricks" had slipped from his mouth a time or two.

His father was a tenured lit professor at San Bernardino Valley College where Parker Jr. was in his last year of study before he would hopefully transfer to a four-year institution. Parker respected his father; he even shared his love for poetry. But it always perplexed Parker as to how his father could preach about the importance of black solidarity and in the next breath wish that "other kinds" of blacks were repopulating the vacancies in the neighborhood. Selah - wasn't the "other kind" of black Mr. Lareaux was looking forward to. She was the "other, other kind" and that's why she believed Parker never invited her to his parents' house until his father's brother died.

The living room was stuffy, like the front door hadn't been opened for more than six seconds at a time since his parents left three days before.

"Only reason you got me over here is because your family's gone, huh?"

Selah placed her elbow on the armrest of the couch and cleared her throat for punctuation.

Parker dropped his gym-slash-book bag by the coffee table and slid into her.

"No, I got you here 'cause this is the only place that is private." He placed his hand on Selah's inner thigh and got it stuck when she clamped her legs shut.

"Damn girl, what you doin'?"

"You better ask a lady. Don't just assume stuff. How you gonna feel if I just start grabbing your crotch?"

"Blessed," he said, and commenced to kiss the outside of her neck.

"Nuh uh, I don't care," she pushed his lips away with the palm of

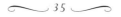

her hand. "You said the reason we weren't going to the library was because you wanted to get out of your sweaty track clothes."

"Ain't like you ain't ever done this in the library. The gym bathroom." He leaned into her neck again.

She shrugged to the left. "Yeah, but I'm in your parents' house now and you know they don't like me."

"They ain't here; what's the problem?"

Selah raised her eyebrows.

"So they *don't* like me?"

Parker leaned back on the couch. "You trippin'. I didn't say nothing like that."

"You said 'They ain't here,' instead of 'They *do* like you.' What you should have said is 'Girl you trippin', my parents *do* like you.'"

Parker looked at Selah like she had lost her last marble. Selah looked back at him and rolled her eyes.

"Baby," he sighed and placed his hand on her thigh, differently this time. "My folks ain't even met you yet."

Selah glared at him to see if he believed what he was saying, then smacked her lips. "Yeah, but look at how your momma treats me when I call, 'Parker *isn't* home.' That's all she says. Crisp and short, like she 'bout to fall off the edge of her words. Like I'm Jigga-boo's daughter something. She don't even ask my name; she just hears my voice and tells me you ain't home."

Parker laughed and rolled his head on the back of the couch.

"It ain't funny, Parker. I didn't do nothin' to your dragon-headed momma."

Parker kept his head on the back of the couch and looked up into the stucco ceiling as he spoke. "Don't you call my momma out of her name unless you call it right. Thunder Thighs Chartreuse."

"*Shar-truce?*"

Parker laughed again. "I guess it has something to do with her being light skinned with green eyes."

"Bet you it's because it sounds high-sidity, 'cause your momma—" she glanced at the painting of his mother over the fireplace, looking all Lena Horne in *Stormy Weather,* wearing a yellow frilly dress. The kind Selah would never let her grandmother make her wear as a child. "I'm 'bout to go home," Selah straightened her skirt and attempted to push up from the couch. He blocked her with his arm.

"You better move your scrawny arm. My grandma told me to never stay anyplace I'm not welcomed."

Parker took in the extra moisture in Selah's eyes.

"You are takin' this way over the viaduct—see." Parker placed one finger on Selah's knee and made a half circle in the air that landed his finger on the third cushion of the couch. "We are really here, but you're taking our conversation all the way over there." He looked back to the far cushion then back at Selah.

"Don't try to make me laugh. I've never known anybody's momma not to like me," she paused, "it just hurts my feelings. I didn't even get a chance to screw up."

"This is the deal," Parker leaned forward over his gapped legs and planted his gym shoes firmly in the blue shag carpet.

"You are my girlfriend, not Glodine's and not my father's. And if they never like you, as long as I do, that's all that matters to me."

Parker held his hands clasped under his chin and stared at Selah like he had never said anything more true in his life. He looked like a man to her, not a boy. A man whose word she could place a pitcher of water on and know it would never fall off.

"Mama Gene warned me you pretty boys were trouble."

Selah took one of his hands in both of hers and sucked the entire day of his index finger into her mouth. She could taste the dirt and tar from the track field under his nails.

Parker knew what she wanted. He pulled her right leg over his lap and began to swirl slow circles in the crotch of her panties. Her left leg trembled. She slouched down with her head tilted back on the couch and opened her legs wider, into a more obtuse angle. Her body let go, and Selah's sandaled foot buckled over into the carpet.

"Like that?" he said, staring at his fingers as moistness appeared like a magic trick through the lining of the lace. He pushed the panties to the side.

"Yeah," she said pensively, "just a little bit harder."

Parker pressed his index and middle fingers deeper into her flesh, but not too far.

"Rub your titties for me, Selah," he said, meeting her eyes, with a look that resembled pain on his face. "You have the most beautiful titties." He watched her closely as she unbuttoned her blouse one button at a time. "I could just put my face between them and suck on 'em all day. Like I was a baby or something."

Parker's words excited her even more, and as she pressed her meaty thighs farther apart, a gush of warmth flowed from her womb.

"You make me smile every time you do that," he said, his smile partially eclipsed by his fingers to his nose.

Selah didn't move. She closed her eyes and concentrated on the full feeling settling over her body.

"You wouldn't believe what I thought while you were doing that," she said sluggishly, her lips forming a lopsided grin.

"What?" he said, the smell of sex and Jean Naté still in his nose.

"I imagined us doing this on the grassy area in the center of the track."

"The football field?"

"Yeah," she said.

"That would be cool. We could sneak out there late on a Saturday night or something."

"Yeah." She imagined what blades of grass would feel like splitting under her skin. If her full behind would stain green from becoming one with Parker on the earth. Selah smoothed her hand down his chest and stuck it into the sweaty waistband of his shorts.

This wasn't about sex. This wasn't about anything strange or abnormal. This was about trust. Trust that only real loving and acceptance opens you up to. They could tell each other anything. Sit under the bleachers and talk about Mama Gene's pills or Parker's mom always harassing him to go to church.

Selah told Parker about what she used to do as a young girl behind the Head Start building trash cans. The small fingers. How she used to pile the quarters onto her bed at night and think about her mother.

"Every time I used to let the boys finger me, I would feel good and bad at the same time." Selah looked into Parker's eyes. "I used to wonder if my mother felt the same way when she was being groped by men she didn't know. Maybe I wanted to be like her." Her forehead muscles frowned reflexively. "So that I wouldn't feel so bad when people said nasty things about her—I'd know she was still a good person because I was." Selah shrugged her shoulders, "sounds strange, huh?"

"Can I share something with you?" Parker asked.

Selah nodded yes, still holding gaze with his eyes.

He didn't judge her. All he did was read her a poem by this Lebanese guy about too many fragments of spirit being scattered and children walking naked with burden and ache. He understood. And this was the first time in her life she cried in front of someone and - didn't feel ashamed.

Something was different about him. He was settled. Nothing was urgent or too lofty in his world. She wanted to learn this from him. How to lay down her cross and not disappear from lack of weight. Selah thought that maybe this gift came from having two parents and a real family. She had looked around his mother's living room and saw pictures of the four of them. Not just family portraits, but candid photos of barbecue picnics and Parker Sr. making mud pies in the backyard with his two boys. Selah didn't have any pictures like this to look back on. She didn't have one memory that she had shared with both of her parents. She had never even met her father, still. And even though they lived in the same city, she never expected to. One person wanting could never make it right for the two.

Selah didn't feel sorry for herself. She had grown up with girls like Carla and Tina Perkins who had less than what she had. Their mothers focused their energies on men maintenance—chasing them, keeping them, staying young. All they had left to give their children was the by-product of freedom. Carla and Tina made Selah feel glad about her rules. At least she knew that Mama Gene loved her, even if hardness was the only way she knew how to show it.

Parker's body shifted into hers as they nodded off on the couch. Selah tilted his shoulder away from her and slid from under him. She crept barefoot through powder blue strings toward the front door. Bending down over her book bag, she unzipped the main compartment.

Parker turned in her direction and blinked his greenish-hazel eyes hard a few times to gain focus.

"What, you trying to steal my baby pictures or something?"

"Something like that," Selah said as she pulled the 35mm camera on loan to her from the photography department out of her bag.

Parker smiled, still dazed from sleep, but aware of what she was doing.

"You may as well put that back, 'cause ain't enough trust in the world."

Selah giggled and lined herself up with him on the opposite side of the coffee table.

"Let me shoot you," Selah said, lifting the camera to her eyes.

Parker placed both hands over his flaccid penis and dangling balls.

"Don't make me break that camera."

Selah giggled harder and jumped up and down three times like she had just scored the highest points on the *Gong Show*.

"Come on, just one picture. It's for my project."

"You need to check yourself into Patton State 'cause all your marbles are gone."

Selah lowered the camera from her face and placed her hand on her hip. The camera hung between the bare mounds of her breasts as she stared at him plain faced.

"Get mad all you want; I'm serious. You are not about to turn my nude, well-hung body into an assignment for any of your little freaky photography professors. They keep copies; I bet you anything."

Selah stood there, hip popped, staring him down.

"Pouting ain't gonna help you," he said, his hand still at attention over his penis.

She smacked her lips. "You sound like my grandmomma. All I want is one picture, Parker. I don't even have to take a picture of your face. You can just pose however you want."

Parker rolled his eyes in the back of his head to think for a second. As soon as Selah felt the pause she knew she was in.

"How do you want to pose?" she said, widening her stance, then focusing the lens of the camera.

Parker thought he was being funny. He placed his socked feet on the couch, lay back, and stacked his hands around his hardening penis like he was strangling it.

Selah snapped.

Chapter Nine

"You smell like an orangatang," Selah mumbled under her breath as she sat in the barely filled bathtub. She took the faded square of cut-up towel, soaked it with water, then swatted it across her back. She wasn't sure why Mama Gene's words embarrassed her so. It had been three hours since Mama Gene had said it, but the sting still pulsed through her cheeks. Selah watched the cloth sink into the V of water between her legs and tried to remember everything she had learned in school. After about twenty minutes, she figured out that orangutan had to be what happened to an orange when it stayed in the refrigerator too long and turned white and black with blue speckles.

"I don't smell like no damn *orangatang,* shoot," Selah said low, her lips half an inch from the water, knowing that Mama Gene would whip her wet legs with a eucalyptus branch if she heard her swearing—whether Ruthie Mae was there or not.

Ruthie Mae slept in Selah's room that night. Even though it was the same room that Ruthie Mae had grown up in, even though it - hadn't changed much in Ruthie's absence, Selah was a little embarrassed by its state. The room wasn't dirty or messy. Selah never left cereal bowls on the dresser or stuffed papers under her bed. It was just a room, plain and ordinary. And Ruthie wearing her tight, solid gold velveteen pants had extended herself worlds beyond this place.

"Mama Gene said she's gonna let me paint the room peach next summer." Selah plopped herself on the bed.

"Is that right?" Ruthie Mae said, her back to Selah. Ruthie's butt swayed back and forth as she looked at Selah's old school pictures taped on the dresser mirror.

"Yeah," Selah said, placing her sweaty hands behind her back. "I might even be able to get a new bed with a brass headboard."

Ruthie picked up a birthday card Mama Gene had given Selah the year before.

"Well, don't hold your breath. This stale green's been chipping off the walls since I was your age."

Selah looked around the room. The paint wasn't chipping. The paint was dull and thin; you could almost see traces of white under it. Maybe that's why Ruthie had to leave Mama Gene's house. She saw something happening that no one else did. Maybe if Selah looked hard enough she could see it, too.

Ruthie plopped herself down on the bed in much the same fashion Selah had. She put her arm over Selah's shoulder and hugged Selah's face to her chest.

"It's amazing you're my little girl. You gotta be strong though, like your momma. Your momma don't take no shit from nobody unless I want to."

Selah half smiled, her hands getting stickier still.

"Do me a favor, Selah Marie."

"Yes, ma'am."

"Yes, ma'am?" Ruthie looked at Selah and rolled her eyes. "Don't you let your grandma's tongue make you a coward, okay? Don't you get embarrassed when she talks to you out the side of her neck, crazy, like she did tonight. You just stand your ground. Don't even talk back, just stand your ground."

"I can do that," Selah said.

Ruthie leaned back on her elbows.

"Can you do me one more favor, Selah?"

"Yes, ma'am—I mean, yeah, Momma."

"Well see, your momma's back is hurting. And your Mama Gene won't give me any of the white pills she takes to help me out. You know the white pills I'm talking about?"

"Maybe. Mama Gene has two different white kinds."

"Okay, you know the bigger one with the line down the middle on one side and a three on the other side?"

"I know that one."

Ruthie sat up and placed her velveteen legs Indian-style on the bed.

"Can you tell me where she keeps them?"

Selah didn't know what to do. Giving Ruthie Mae the pills would violate the pact she had with Papa Frank. It wouldn't have been so serious if Papa Frank and Selah had a normal relationship, but they didn't. Papa Frank stayed out of Selah's way to the point that he never touched her. Selah knew that this separation had everything to do with Ruthie Mae. Ruthie Mae had been what most folks would have called a *fast kid*. Ruthie always wanted to be in grown folks' faces, especially men. And if Ruthie didn't get her way, she would lie. Big, hurtful, make-Mama-Gene-wanna-knife-somebody-over-messing-with-her-child kind of lies. Ruthie had told these kind of lies on Papa Frank, and Selah, though she looked and acted nothing like her mother, inherited the fallout.

"I'm supposed to give the pills to Papa Frank when I find 'em."

"What?" Ruthie wrinkled her forehead.

"If I find any of Mama Gene's pills, I'm supposed to hide 'em in my room and give 'em to Papa Frank when Mama Gene ain't around."

"You got some right now, Selah?" Ruthie touched the outside of Selah's shoulder.

Selah was hesitant.

"Selah, I'm your momma. You're not supposed to lie or hold things back from your momma."

Selah felt bad.

"I have three of 'em. I found them in the kitchen mixed in with the flour." Selah had really found ten. But if Momma Ruthie loved the pill anywhere near as much as Mama Gene did, all of them would be gone before morning.

"Good girl, get up and get them for your momma, would you."

Selah went into her closet and dug three pills out of the side pocket of her school satchel.

"Here," she said, handing them to Ruthie on her sticky palm.

"Now go get your momma a glass of Kool-Aid."

When Selah got back, Ruthie was under the thin comforter on Selah's bed with the bed's one pillow tucked behind her back. She had on one of Papa Frank's plain white V-neck T-shirts that Mama Gene had given her. Selah handed Ruthie the water.

"All the Kool-Aid is gone." Selah sat at the end of the bed. "Momma, can you do me a favor and not tell anyone I gave you the pills?"

Ruthie gulped all three down with the faucet water.

"You afraid of ole evil Papa Frank?"

Selah nodded her head yes.

"Don't worry, he's more afraid of me." She laughed and Selah - didn't like the sound. It was the infected laugh of someone who knew too much. Selah had never been able to put her finger on the distance between her and Papa Frank, why he never hugged her or let Selah play on his lap. Now she knew for sure that Ruthie was the reason.

"I'll make me a pallet on the floor."

"Girl, just put on your gown and hop in."

"I woulda put it on already but I left it in here when I took my bath."

Ruthie rolled her eyes. "You put that filthy shirt and those shorts back on? Are you afraid of me seeing you change?"

Selah shrugged her shoulders.

"Get over there and put on your gown," Ruthie nudged her toward the dresser. Everything you got, I already have; I ain't studying you."

When Selah settled into bed with her mother, she got the spot next to the wall on the smaller end of the pillow. She felt the heat of her mother's arm and leg touching hers.

"Mama Gene says that I'm a wild sleeper."

"You ain't no wilder than me," Ruthie laughed.

"You still see my father," Selah folded her sweaty hands into her nylon gown.

Ruthie Mae breathed in hard. Selah felt her chest drop when she let the air go.

"Yes, Selah, I still see your father." Ruthie let out another breath.

"Does he know about me?"

Ruthie tapped her fingernail a few times on her chest.

"He basically knows about you. He knows you live here with my mother."

"Does he know my name?"

"He's heard your name here and there. He even saw your kindie-garden picture once."

Once, Selah thought to herself. Like something you keep in a junk drawer and come across accidentally. Once. Kindergarten was three years ago. Selah was about to go into the third grade.

Selah turned on her stomach and looked at her mother.

"You live with 'um?"

"Basically."

"You love 'um, Ruthie Mae, I mean Momma Ruthie. You love 'um?"

"Like God loves the devil. Sometimes things just get out of control. Wish I didn't even know his black ass sometimes. Humph."

"Is he nice to you?" Selah asked.

"Um, hmm. He's always nice when he wants something."

Ruthie looked at Selah for the first time in minutes. Selah paused and looked into the dark brown eyes of her mother. One day when Selah got older she would recall this day and draw cat lines around her own eyelids with a black-brown Maybelline liner pencil.

"He doesn't want to see me, does he?"

There was no way to answer what men like him thought to do with young girls. Ruthie Mae had been fourteen when she met him.

"You just full of questions, ain't you? Save something for next time, you gonna have to let me get some sleep."

Selah watched Ruthie sleep that night. She noticed that her eyes jumped under their lids every few seconds and that slobber gathered in the corners of her mouth but never dried down the sides of her face like Selah's did most nights. She wondered if Ruthie felt good sleeping next to her. If she wanted to be there or if this was a necessary pit stop on her way to somewhere else. The only thing Selah did know was that Ruthie would leave, she always did. Selah lay there with her head resting on her arm, staring at her mother's sleeping, made-up face, sucking the last of the pomegranate and dirt juice from under her nails. She didn't know why she felt this way, but she wasn't sure she wanted Ruthie to stay. Selah learned things she didn't want to know when Ruthie was around—like she would never have a dad, and all she could ever hope for from Ruthie was sometimes. When Ruthie left the next morning she took away the magic of her gold velveteen pants and the mystery of Selah's father. She took the seven pills from Selah's school bag and Selah's second grade school picture from the dresser mirror. Selah was left alone, in a twin bed that now seemed strangely too big, wondering if this was the type of mother she would be when she had a child.

Chapter Ten

Selah would sit cross-legged like she usually did, back of knees sweating through coffee-colored nylon pantyhose. She was still nervous being in the house of The Lord, like though the doors of the church were open to anyone, God hadn't invited her. She wanted to sneak in under His radar. That's why she showed up early, knowing that God noticed latecomers more—so did the rest of the congregation.

Although most of the Bible study sessions were held in off-shoot classrooms, three classes were being held in various parts of the sanctuary when she first walked in. Selah went to the far left aisle and found a seat on the end of the tenth pew. The tenth row gave her just enough distance to watch Parker like a hawk. It also positioned her under the almost cool breeze of the swamp cooler harnessed near the ceiling. Selah always joked with herself that the reason she - didn't attend church more regularly was because black churches - didn't believe in centralized air conditioning. She giggled under her breath, the kind that can only be heard on the inside of yourself. In her heart, she knew her absence from church had nothing to do with the heat that most churches propagated, but rather with reasons she rarely allowed herself to think of.

As the choir director warmed up the piano, playing shout and stomp music to an empty choir stand, Selah grabbed a Bible from the back of the pew in front of her. She looked down the row and noticed that each holder attached to the back of the seats was stocked with a hardcover Bible, hymn book, and two offering envelopes. The hymn books were new, she thought, so was the fluffy mauve carpeting. Selah flicked the snakeskin slingback off of her right foot and pressed the ball into the carpet. The arch of her foot began to let go of the tension that mounted whenever she wore heels higher than two inches, which was most of the time.

Selah stared into the vastness of the church. The church seemed divided to her. The apexes of the ceiling and the walls were predominantly white, while eye level, from the pews to the pulpit, everything was brown. She looked up again into the sharp angles of the ceiling. She felt small here. Smaller than she ever felt anywhere else. She breathed in. The stained-glass depiction of Jesus ascending from the grave into a blue, red, and yellow sky caught her attention. A white beveled-glass sash draped his waist. At least Jesus was brown, she smirked, having seen so many depictions of a blond-haired, pale-skinned Jesus in black churches. She liked the idea of Jesus being in her image. The cinnamon-black tones of his stained-glass skin made her feel more at peace, like maybe she and Jesus had more in common than she thought.

Her mind drifted back to Parker. Soon he would make his way to the center pew, third row. She was proud of the way he looked in his black suit, how it rounded his thin shoulders and coated his long body with a layer of authority. She trusted him, though she basically didn't have to. Everything that could have happened in their marriage had already happened. Selah wasn't afraid of being betrayed by stray actions any more. She was afraid of not knowing about them. And this was part of the problem: Whereas Parker preferred not to know about anything contrary to what he wanted for himself and his wife, Selah needed to know. The thirst to find Parker unfaithful in any way drove her, and that's why she made her sporadic visits to Mount Calvary Church, where Parker Lareaux had been a deacon for ten years and was now studying to become a minister.

Parker was a faithful man; any clue Selah found that hinted otherwise was an illusionary hope. But to soothe her own tired conscience, she looked in the only place Parker had to hide such a thing: the church. She didn't want him to cheat. But if he did, just once, maybe he would understand her better. Maybe she wouldn't feel so bad about her own indiscretions.

Her visits were always impromptu, meaning Parker didn't know about them until he noticed Selah's face in a string of church hats and shaped cardboard fans. She would watch him dress and get ready for Bible study, she'd let him kiss her good-bye and tell her he wouldn't make it home until after two. As soon as she heard his idling engine shift into reverse in the driveway, she'd calmly flip the comforter from over her legs, take a pressed suit, pantyhose, and matching shoes from the closet, and get dressed. Selah always dressed sharp for church. There'd even been occasions she'd bought a suit for the sole purpose of wearing it to service. She found that a polished exterior soothed the discomfort of clapping along and mouthing the words to gospel songs she'd never learned as a child.

•   •   •

Selah's Bed

The sanctuary started to fill.

Selah slipped her size ten slingback back onto her foot. She paid close attention to the people walking past, especially the women. There was a holy look to churchwomen that mystified Selah. It was something on the inside of them that shined past the fitted skirts and brightly colored hairdos. She wondered if it was forgiveness that separated her from them. Selah took inventory of who sat next to whom and who stared a little too long at sister *proud breasts* or brother *gotta wife*. She wished that she could consider herself a holy woman. The kind that cooked Sunday dinner for the family and never showed any skin above the knee, not even in bed. Selah would only allow herself brief moments of thoughts like these. She'd shake her head and laugh on the inside about how boring normalcy and wholeness would be. She had an exciting life. A life riddled with spontaneous interactions and nonrenewable moments. She thought about this instead as the church band kicked into the same drum and piano heavy rhythm she'd heard in every church she'd been to in her entire life.

As members continued to arrive and Bible study participants emptied from classrooms into the sanctuary, the mood of the sanctuary grew more vibrant with Sunday morning chatter. Mount Calvary seated about five hundred people and had a membership of about the same. Because of the size of some members and others who occupied two seats—one with themselves and the other with their purses and Bibles—the church had an eight o'clock and an eleven o'clock service each Sunday. The church pews had been donated five years ago by Dr. Paul and Bernice Rhodes, just weeks before Dr. Rhodes's death. The pews were made of mahogany wood and the center row started about twenty feet from the pulpit, going twenty rows deep. Either side of the church held fifteen rows, each pew faced slightly inward with a brass plate on its side that said, IN APPRECIATION, DR. AND MRS. PAUL RHODES.

Selah looked around the church again, this time for familiar faces. It wasn't that she knew anyone in the church or that anyone knew her; any familiarity had been garnered over the years through brief introductions and stories Parker shared every so often. Selah picked out Mother Jackson, Pastor Jackson's mother, wearing a pink, netted hat with white gloves. Who Selah was really looking for was Cathy Jean James—in all her manipulative, church-going, husband-hunting splendor. Parker had mentioned Cathy Jean's name just a few times too many for Selah to be comfortable with the woman being around her husband. Of course there was always a good reason for Cathy Jean to be in Parker's face—problems with her son, her mother, her *anything* that she thought would get Parker's attention. Selah's favorite instance had to be on Minister Appreciation Sunday when Cathy Jean called the house before church, crying. Parker raced out like usual. Met her at Denny's on Jefferson near Sepulveda only to find out that Cathy Jean had this dream in which *God* revealed to her that she and Parker were supposed to be together.

"God *revealed* this to me, Parker, and I can see that you are not as happy as you could be," she said, then squeezed his hand in support. There was a part of Parker that was flattered by this desperate attention; Selah thought it was disgusting.

"People are human, Selah," he told her, "sometimes the most wrong desires can feel like God if you want them bad enough." Parker smiled and touched Selah's hand much the way she imagined Cathy Jean had touched his hand that morning. The same way Selah would touch another man's body that night.

Reverend Jackson entered from the door just east of the choir stand and took his seat on a crushed velvet chair next to three other ministers. Minister Todd, all of five feet five inches in a deep purple suit, stood and walked to the podium.

"Will the congregation pleeeze stand."

With a ripple effect, the congregation placed their Bibles and belongings to the side and stood up. Selah stood and held on tightly to the back of the pew in front of her. She closed her eyes out of nervousness before Minister Todd asked them to. It felt like everyone's eyes were on her, including God's. With heels on, her six-foot stature made her feel spotlighted. She kept her eyes closed, anticipating the moment when she would be able to sit down.

Every eye closed, every head bowed . . . "Let us pray. Lawd-da, we thank you for the ability to appear in your presence this mornin-na. We ask that you allow your son Jeeez-us to be with us today, dear Lawd-da. That you lose your holy spirit in our midst, Lawd. That you would bind everything that is not like you, Lawd . . ."

That you end this prayer and let us to sit down, Lawd-da, Selah said under her breath.

". . . Please allow us to be sound vessels for your word, Lawd. That you would forgive us of our trespasses, sweet, sweet, Jeeez-us. Please bless Reverend Jackson as he brings forth your message, Hallelujah Jeeez-us. Bless the teachin' and the hearin' of your word, Lawd. And we will praaaise ya Jeeez-us. You are wooorthyy Lawd. Hallelujah. Hallelujah. And let the congregation say. Amen and Amen."

Clearly the woman next to Selah had caught the spirit early. Selah knew this because of the way her floral skirt moved back and forth rhythmically, like the center piece of a metronome. When the rest of the congregation took their collective seat, the woman stood there, her arms outstretched, her palms arched hard toward heaven. Every so often Selah heard versions of "Yes, Lord, have your way

Jesus," and some other language she couldn't understand. Sometimes when Parker didn't realize Selah was around the house, she'd
come in from her backyard studio and catch him on the living room
floor, pillows tucked under his knees, face bowed to the carpet,
speaking the same language. The tongues scared her: Not the fact
that she couldn't understand them, but that she didn't understand
the source from which they came. Parker would kneel there, his
mouth expelling words with focused energy into the beige carpet.
Even the way his mouth moved was strange to Selah. She'd watch
the profile of his lips—the way they stretched and puckered swiftly,
yet distinctly over each word, his voice raising and lowering in rhythmic intervals.

It occurred to Selah that Parker was the vessel, not the originator
of the words. Parker was being dictated to by God. He didn't have to
think about what he was saying as he had to in a conversation; he just
had to commit. And Parker committed fluidly to God. God used the
full extension of his tongue, the deepest arch of his back. His tail-
bone, the whitened, overextended balls of his feet. Selah would dis-
miss herself from this image of her prostrated husband and walk
upstairs wondering how she and Parker could have grown so far
apart. How their passions could exhibit themselves so differently.
Selah committed to sex the way Parker committed to God. She
would let go of her backbone during sex. She'd use all her gritty and
guts to chime herself around a penis like a rainbow when she climaxed. This was the only holy water she knew.

After announcements and before the choir in white and royal blue
robes stood to sing "Nearer to Thee Sweet Jesus," Selah noticed
Cathy Jean entering the sanctuary from the prayer room with none
other than Parker following closely behind her. Parker stopped just
short of the pulpit near the offering table while Cathy Jean moved

quickly past four sets of skirted knees into a seat in the ninth row, three arm lengths from Selah's foot up her ass. Selah examined Cathy Jean as she wiped her eyes with a peach handkerchief. Pathetic. Selah hated when women threw themselves on men out of powerlessness. Selah felt that a woman was always supposed to be in control. That women who didn't know this gave the ones who did a bad name. And Cathy Jean wasn't in control. Selah could smell it in the air around her. Cathy Jean wanted Parker with the same tight ache between her thighs as Selah did when she met him her first year of college. She didn't hear the choir's first or second selection. She didn't notice the way Pastor Jackson inflected his voice as he talked about the evils of envy and bones waxing old through silence. She poured all of her attention into Cathy Jean. How she finished off her tears, folded the peach handkerchief into a neat square, and placed it into her jacket pocket. How she hugged the woman next to her and complimented her on the color of her dress. How she exchanged the details of her week just under her breath. This observation process was about principle, not fear. Selah reached into her purse locating a small notepad and pen. She tapped the woman next to her and asked her to pass a note down to Cathy Jean. The small sheet of white paper folded in half with Cathy Jean's name on the outside in cursive writing passed through two hands and was handed to Cathy Jean over her shoulder. Selah watched Cathy Jean's head lower and her eyes focus into the note:

Stay the fuck away from my husband.

Cathy Jean looked confused and turned in both directions to find the source of the note. When her eyes met Selah's, Selah nodded an acknowledgment and smiled kindly to Cathy Jean.

"Good to see you again, Sister James." Selah said, nodded once more, then focused her energy on the pulpit. Selah was pleased with herself. She prided herself on knowing. Knowing when to step in, when to leave something alone. This timing was perfect. She had never felt so integrated in church. This was the first time she felt that she had expressed her true self. And when Parker passed the brass plate for the second offering, Cathy Jean looked in the opposite direction while Selah placed her envelope on top of the others and smiled to him like a good Christian woman.

Chapter Eleven

Selah remembered going to a feet-washing service when she was twelve. Mama Gene bought her a new dress so that Zettie Backstead's daughter L. Nicole wouldn't *outdo* Selah. Zettie Backstead lived in an area of San Bernardino that years later would break away and become its own city, but for now, it was called "you know, over there, where those rich white folks live." Mama Gene had never been to Zettie's house; she'd just heard of its fine details so repetitiously that she felt as though she had been. The petite Italian fountain just inside the front gate, the grand foyer, the lambskin couches dyed to mimic tiger skin.

"My husband just loves hunting," Zettie Backstead said out of nowhere while the other nurses were deciding where to order lunch from. "If he could earn a tiger's head in one of those countries like Africa or something, it would mean the life of him."

Mama Gene shook her head, but only on the inside. If the woman, as tar black as she was, wanted to make the entire continent a country, let her do as she damned well pleased. Mama Gene didn't give an ox's balls about that woman or her husband who played alabaster with a nose just a little too broad to be white. All Mama Gene cared about was her job. And she would go to as many feet washings at Zettie Backstead's whitified singing church as she had to to keep it.

This was the first time Mama Gene had gotten caught stealing pills. She had taken them before, usually before administering meds. It was easy. One for the patient, one for her. Two for her, two plain white aspirin for the patient. The patients were old and most of them ended up in mid- to low-functioning nursing homes because that's what their Medicare afforded.

Mama Gene's preference was to make her rounds then take her lunch hour. That would give her time to eat and acclimate to her high before returning to work. She never knew how Zettie figured it out, maybe Zettie was even calling her bluff, but Mama Gene, Eugenia Wells, LVN, couldn't chance it.

"Eugenia, may I see you in my office?"

Mama Gene asked LaVerne, a Filipino woman on her shift, to finish passing out the meds. Mama Gene knew something was wrong. The bubbly was missing from Zettie's voice and a stern cautiousness replaced it. Zettie never used her office; it was a stuffy cupboard where she housed her briefcase and took private phone calls. Zettie Backstead liked to pretend to be one of the girls, though she and her husband owned two other nursing homes within ten minutes of Sherborne.

Two chairs were pulled out in front of Zettie's desk. Mama Gene squeezed her behind, left side, then right, into the too-tight chair with metal armrests and placed her hands in her lap.

"Eugenia," Zettie closed her eyes hard. "I'm concerned, that's the first thing I need to say. You've been a hard-working employee for me and I am enriched by knowing you."

Mama Gene nodded.

"Here's the problem, Eugenia. I've gotten complaints from several patients that they haven't gotten their painkillers during certain shifts. Do you know anything about this?"

"No, I can't say that I do, Mrs. Backstead."

"Eugenia," Zettie paused and stared Mama Gene soundly in the eye. "I have a witness. I can call a search or we can cut all of this and you can tell me the truth." Zettie leaned back in her chair.

Mama Gene had to think. She still had seven pills in her uniform pocket, three of which she had planned to take during lunch.

"I have to say," Mama Gene said slowly, her voice not wavering a tinge off course, "I am truly, truly sorry for violating your trust."

"Eugenia," a look of deep disappointment spread on Zettie's face. "Whew, I never expected this from you. Didn't you think I'd find out? What about your patients' welfare?"

"I'm sorry, Mrs. Backstead. I'll do whatever I have to do, but I can't lose this job. I support my grandbaby and I need this money. I'll go through probation or whatever. Please." Mama Gene's eyes were sincere.

Zettie leaned forward. "Can I ask you something?"

"Yes, Mrs. Backstead."

"Do you have a relationship with God?"

"Yes, I do believe I do."

"Are you saved by the spirit and washed in the blood?"

Mama Gene shook her head. "I'm not saying all that. I'm saying I know that God, Jesus if you will, does a lot in my life and I'm glad he cares enough to do it."

Zettie shook her head yes as if saying she understood all the shades of what Mama Gene had said.

"Would you like to come to church with me tonight?"

She didn't want to go.

"Yes," Mama Gene said.

"It's a mixed congregation and after Bible study tonight, we are having a feet-washing. It should be special."

"What about my job, Zettie?"

Zettie tightened the beige silk scarf around her neck.

"Take a few days, Eugenia. No need to clean out your locker. I'll pick you up tonight, your address is in my file, and we will talk about all of this on Monday when the path will be clearer."

"I'll see you tonight," Mama Gene said as she fought her way out of the chair. She retrieved her purse from her locker and caught the bus home three blocks down from where she normally did in front of Sherborne Convalescent. And as she sat unshaded in the midday sun, she thought about the seven pills in her pocket and how she had cost herself so much more than three days of no pay.

Selah looked at herself in the paneled mirror of the curtained JCPenney's dressing room.

"It's ugly," Selah said, not looking up at Mama Gene. Selah had only been to one funeral in her life, Papa Frank's mother's, and all she could think was that the dress looked frilly and slippery just like the inside of the coffin.

"Stand straight," Mama Gene commanded.

Selah wouldn't—she didn't care if Mama Gene lit her little butt on fire with her shoe, Selah wasn't going to help make that dress look good.

Mama Gene adjusted the dress on Selah's slouching body, uncuffed the lace around the upper arm, and tied the bow tight and centered on Selah's back.

"See," Mama Gene said, "the dress makes you look ladylike."

"It makes me look like the inside of a coffin, Mama Gene. And the arms are too tight and I hate pink and ribbons and stuff."

Mama Gene snatched Selah's arm and turned Selah back toward the mirror.

"Don't you want to look nice like Zettie's daughter? Zettie's daughter is going to have on ribbons and lacy things, don't you want to fit in?"

Hell no she didn't want to fit in. What would Tina and Tasha-Marie think if they saw all hundred and twelve pounds of her in a little girl dress. Selah started doing the antsy dance, shaking her arms and rolling her head around like it was barely connected to her neck.

"Selah, stop it."

"No, Momma, you gonna make me look ugly, it's too tight, I don't fit little girls' clothes no more. I'm too big." Selah danced around some more.

"Look like the bottom of a clothes hamper then; I'm not studying you."

Selah tried to reach the zipper in the center of her back by herself. Mama Gene snatched the zipper down.

"Don't you want to go to church sometimes like other kids?"

"Not really," she said, grateful that Mama Gene hadn't brought in tights for her to try on.

"Don't you want to know God, Selah?"

She wanted to leave the dress on the ground to show her disdain, but that would have made Mama Gene angrier. She began to place the lightly petticoated monstrosity on the hanger.

"Only if He wants to know me, I guess."

Selah looked Mama Gene in the eyes when she said it. She was sincere about what she had said. God could be her friend like Tina and Carla and Tasha-Marie were. Selah had never turned down a friend. Mama Gene didn't know whether to laugh or cry. Instead, she grabbed Selah to her, wiped her thumb over her tongue, and tamed the wild hairs of Selah's eyebrows.

Chapter Twelve

The first and only time Parker found Selah with another lover, she had forgotten to lock the studio door. She knew she was going to see him. In the way you know things you don't want to believe. In the way you know a glass of milk is a glass of milk—from the color and taste. It came to her early that morning: *Parker will be in the village today.*

Selah filled the half-empty glass of orange juice with tap water and watched its constitution change from cloudy to clear. After drying the last of the morning dishes, she placed plastic wrap over the salmon croquette patty and crinkle of bacon left sitting in a saucer on the stove. Her spirit must have gotten something crossed. *Parker never comes to the village,* she reasoned as she made her way down the hill. Even though Leimert Park was only five minutes from their Windsor Hills home, Parker had been to her studio twice in the last eight years: Once to check out the building before it went into escrow and the second time to attend her opening.

Selah realized that her art was the reason Parker stayed away. Her photographs were an embarrassment to him. He couldn't stand to look at them or be in the same room. On the few occasions she framed works in the main house, before the guesthouse was converted into a workspace, she would hear him mumbling prayers under his breath as he passed from the kitchen through the dining room. Fervent prayers that made her feel like he was trying to cast the photography incubus out of her. She didn't blame him. Parker - didn't understand why a woman, his wife, needed to photograph nude men for a living. To make peace, she hid her work from him. Clients were always scheduled for shoots when he wasn't home, and she never displayed any of her pieces around the house.

This wounded Selah, the way Parker hated the best part of her. How could she explain that the men were giving her the same thing she gave them—peace. Even if the peace was temporary, even if God sealed it off from her the moment they left her presence. She never violated any of them. No one had ever asked for their pieces to not be displayed. She did something different and that's what made her work feel like magic. She captured hurt in a way that it explained itself. And joy so that it seemed like the soft spot on a baby's head. These pictures were the closest she had ever gotten to the truth about anything, especially herself. And if no one else understood that, if Parker never came around, she knew her intention.

That's why Selah had never slept with a client. She wanted something in her life to be pure. And if not pure, good. She had messed up so many times with Parker already. She put no excuse on top of it. She didn't try to make cheating right by telling herself it was okay. It wasn't okay. It wasn't good. She was Parker's wife, a broken one with insides that galvanized under hands that usually had regrets of their own. Her lovers were part of her underworld. Part of the dark spot on the inside of herself that needed loving despite its imperfection.

Like any addiction, like anything you pour yourself into to get away from yourself, the *When's* and *Why's* of how she met this man who Parker found in her bed didn't matter to Selah. She could have met him buying the same brand of film at Costco or he could have offered to carry out the bag of ice she bought at 7-Eleven. The only thing that was important was that he could travail her darkness without looking away.

Normally, she would have locked the door. The possibility of Parker seeing her breasts in another man's mouth would have flashed in her head and she would have locked the deadbolt, too. But this - wasn't one of those days. This wasn't a day when she committed clearly to her sin and walked a straight line into this man's arms. All she had thought about this day was her daughter. Michelle. And it was the dullness of the ache that had brought her to the upper room.

Selah sat on the bed. Her back hunched over, her spine leaving a curve of sweat against the wall. She had it wrong. The feeling never started in her throat. The ache in her throat was because of her bottom lip—the way it trembled, how it gave way to rumbling that caught at the base of her gums and traveled back under the tongue. If she could just stop the trembling, the rumble wouldn't catch and then the keening couldn't come. And if the keening never started, she didn't have to think about Michelle. She didn't have to sit in the stale bed again with her toes dug into musty sheets and recount memories that never yielded an answer. Selah reminded herself to think about this next time. She was already here now.

I miss you Michelle. And it hurts. I'm so angry, I can't even cry. I try to cry. I try to force the feelings out of my eyes but they won't come. Neither will you.

· · ·

Maybe the tears would never come, but the sex was a way out. Selah sat facing him on his lap, her body concave around him. She imagined he was the Sit and Spin she used to have when she was five. It had a round plastic base and a column sticking out of the center with a six-inch dial on top. She used to wrap her legs around the column and spin hard. The faster she turned the dial, the faster she whipped around.

Selah didn't know when Parker walked in. She didn't hear the bottom of the door grate the loose metal plate on the carpet as it was pushed open. All she noticed was that a few moments before she climaxed, she smelled the freshness of his cologne. When she looked up, he was there. In the same tan no-wrinkle slacks and beige short-sleeve shirt he had worn out of the house that morning. His Boeing aircraft badge with photo I.D. was clipped to his belt. Selah fought the wave. She tried to still her body quickly so that she could speak. Parker spoke first.

"Help me Jesus," is all he said. There were to be no arguments or issuance of ultimatums. They would not cry and hold each other until the quaking stopped. There would just be silent breakfasts together and loud prayer that Selah would notice late nights when she was supposed to be sleeping.

Chapter Thirteen

Bathing Mama Gene reminded Selah of the time she made Selah get her feet washed at church. Selah ended up wearing a pair of jeans with a raised topstitch traveling up the center of her leg, around half of her behind, and down the other side with a dark green V-neck T-shirt and sandals that caused her to slip on the splitting heel when she walked too fast. Mama Gene shook her head as Selah sauntered past on the way to the couch. Selah saw Mama Gene's lip flare up toward her nose in her peripheral vision, and all of a sudden the pot roast and smothered potato smell permeating the apartment's early evening air didn't seem as attractive.

"You want something to eat?"

Selah propped her heel against the linoleum so that her toes pointed toward the ceiling. She squeezed her foot hard against the fake leather lining of her sandal trying to see how far the heel could split from its other half before it broke away.

"You gonna break that sandal, Selah, and I can't wait to throw the damned things in the trash can."

Sister Wells, what fine church language you have this evening, Selah thought but wouldn't dare say to her grandmother. Selah giggled low.

"I ain't hungry, Mama Gene."

"Okay, don't get to sitting in some long, boring service talking 'bout your stomach hurts. I ain't gonna hear it. One night without dinner ain't gonna kill you no how."

Selah adjusted the heel of her sandal back onto the rest of her shoe and walked toward the kitchen.

"Take this plate for me, would you please." Mama Gene leaned back from the table and let out a breath.

Selah picked up Mama Gene's plate in her right hand and threw the paper towel and all into the sink. She removed the thick lid from the cast-iron skillet and a moist steam of garlic, onion powder, and - Lawry's hit her face. Selah stepped back one step then reached across the aisle to grab a plate. As she tore through the tender brown flesh with her fork, she felt betrayed by Mama Gene. How could Mama Gene now start saying that missing one meal wouldn't kill her? Selah had become the Pavlovian dog of eating. Any time a pleasant smell rose from her grandmother's kitchen, she had been trained to get up and get some, even if she had smelled it in her sleep. Even if she went right back to sleep after she ate. Selah stuck her fork into two potatoes then smothered the whole lot in gravy thinking all the while about how she wore husky clothing and was never the same size as her friends.

She sat across from Mama Gene at the oblong veneered wood table. Mama Gene was wearing her best brown linen suit with a complementary netted hat that covered the slightest bit of her ginger brown forehead. Selah liked how Mama Gene laughed big and gapped-toothed when she wore that outfit. She wished her grandmother would wear White Shoulders and that outfit every day. Things would be different if she did, maybe she wouldn't need the pills so much.

Selah's Bed

Mama Gene flipped through the pages of a Bible that looked new, but had been sitting on Mama Gene's nightstand for at least six years. Selah had never seen Mama Gene look through the Bible before. Selah wondered what she was trying to find. She flipped peacefully and unrushed.

Whenever Selah recalled a time in her life where Mama Gene looked beautiful, this was the image she would always return to.

On the ride to the church, Zettie was sure to explain from the burgundy leather pulpit of her Volvo that *L. Nicole* was short for Lossietta Nicole, but because her daughter didn't like the amount of syllables in her name, she and her husband got it legally changed to *L.* when she was ten. Selah knew that Mama Gene was gonna curse this woman purple behind her back for changing a ten-year-old - child's name. *I wish I would.* Selah could hear Mama Gene's mouth already. She glanced over at L. Nicole. Selah had never known a little girl to have so much power. She wanted to touch the blondish brown hair on the girl's skinny arm to see if she felt any different than the other little girls Selah knew.

All of the women who washed feet sat on their knees in front of a row of twenty brown metal fold-up chairs with a square ten-quart bucket of warm salted water and two towels placed at their knees. The washings were done in shifts. After the men dismissed themselves, the women formed a line of less than seventy women down the right aisle of the church facing the pulpit.

Selah and Mama Gene were in the second batch of women to go; Zettie and her fourteen-year-old daughter, L. Nicole, helped to wash feet.

Mama Gene got placed first and Selah got a seat a few minutes later beside a woman with blotchy liver-spotted feet. Selah wanted to let the woman in back of her go first, but she didn't feel like getting a spanking in church for disrespecting her grandmother twice in one day.

Selah took off her raggedy sandals and placed them under her chair. A white woman with short auburn waves and a smile of a thousand little teeth washed her feet.

"My grandma wears that perfume," Selah said to the woman as she pulled Selah's feet, toes first, into the salt bath. Nancy Sue Ellen sponged the rag heavy with water over Selah's feet. *This is what special is supposed to feel like,* Selah thought. She glanced over at Mama Gene. Mama Gene held her eyes closed with her chin pointed down toward the swamp of her chest. Selah knew her grandmother was relaxed because her knees buckled outward, arcing away from each other. The woman on her knees in front of Mama Gene washed her feet diligently, like they were her own mother's feet—gentle and firm, in broad circular movements. Years later, Selah would wash Mama Gene's entire body the same way and recall this foot washing, wondering if there'd be anyone to sponge down her own body when it was time.

Chapter Fourteen

It wasn't that they were strangers. They weren't strangers. They knew each other, down to the discolored parts of each other's skin and how long a blackhead took to gestate on each other's backs.

Selah was still a wife to Parker. A wife in all the expected ways that someone would miss first if the services were stopped. She still made breakfast on Saturday morning and dinner twice a week even if it was leftovers from the deep freezer. She still cared that he loved her salmon croquette and hated his eggs runny. When Selah did have to borrow Parker's car, she never left the plastic root beer bottle in his cup holder or forgot to throw away the empty red super-sized french fry container wedged between the driver's seat and the gear box.

Parker provided similar services. Every time he washed his own car he was sure to wash Selah's and he always called when he was coming home late even if they had no mutual plans for the evening. The Lareauxs had a peaceful existence. They didn't argue very often or fuss about the little things. Both of them knew that they couldn't. Both of them knew that there was seriousness lurking under their kindness and immense need for household order.

Even their sex had become orderly. *Back sex,* Selah called it. Back sex, bed sex, morning sex, night sex. She hated the formula of their connection. It used to be different. They used to use every part of the house. The dishwasher, the bathroom floor. Some of the best sex they'd ever had had been in the dirt under the bleachers Selah's first year of college. Selah remembered going home with a coat of dirt and small rocks in her ruffled, pressed hair, the thick pomade acting as glue. The more she tried to shake and pat the dirt out, the deeper it penetrated. Selah appreciated the dirt though. She appreciated that she had wanted Parker enough not to stop him when her head slid off his San Bernardino High School letterman's jacket onto the dusty hard-as-concrete ground. Selah always blamed Parker jokingly for the fragile spot of hair in the back of her head that never grew back properly after that incident. But Selah didn't mind that— or the thin scratches on her behind, or skin off of both of her elbows. These things were all counted as war wounds that the best sex opened you up to.

Selah couldn't recall when, but they had left the good stuff alone years ago—after Michelle and before the affairs, between no more kids and a house too big for the two of them.

"Will you stop it, Selah," Parker said, flagging her out of his study.

Selah glanced over the big, blue, heavy concordance and multiple yellow pads steeped in Parker's scribbly cursive writing.

"Tell me you don't ever think about it then," Selah said, popping a squat on the loveseat, which served as Parker's bed most nights.

"Selah, baby, this is my study time. Please."

Selah's Bed

"That's exactly what I'm talking about, Parker. Your study time, your prayer time, your church time, your deacon meeting time, your new member outreach phone call time. And you're telling me the truth when you say that you don't think that God is interfering in our relationship? *Please* yourself."

"Selah, I really don't understand how you could have been raised to twist your mouth this way. *God* is the reason you are here."

She wasn't going to let him turn this on her. He wanted her to be disappointed in herself, to break down and ask for forgiveness for speaking what she felt to be true.

"Parker, just because I wasn't raised having to go to church every five minutes like you were doesn't mean that I don't have any under-standing of God. Isn't there somewhere in the Bible where it talks about honoring your wife as your self? Isn't *that* somewhere in your Bible?"

Selah tapped her foot. The energy was building up in her hip socket and tapping was the only way she knew to let it go besides running or sex.

Parker leaned back into his chair and spoke in a depressed tone. "Ephesians, chapter five, verse twenty-eight, Selah," he shook his head, "but—"

"No *but,* Parker, that's what it says." She slapped both of her legs to signal the end of the conversation.

"It also says, Selah, that no man has ever hated his own flesh and he nourishes it and cherishes it as *God* does the church. For we are members of his flesh and bone—"

"You make me sick, Parker."

"And what about First Peter, chapter three, verse seven, Selah? Yes. It says for husbands to give honor to their wives as the weaker vessel and not to allow their prayers to be hindered."

"It also says," Selah chimed in, knowing that Parker would be surprised that she had put time into having a rebuttal for him this time, "it also says for husbands to love their wives and not to be bitter against them."

Parker smiled in amusement and hunched himself back over his books. "And it also says it is good for a man not to touch a woman." Parker laughed to himself, hoping that his poke was slight enough for Selah to overlook.

"I don't even know why I deal with you. If you don't want to have sex with me you don't have to, *ever*."

"Baby," he pinched the bridge of his nose, "why do you always have to take things too far?"

Selah frowned her lips in the stinking lip pose like Mama Gene, but didn't say anything.

"I want to have sex with you, Selah, just not during my God time and just not—"

"And just not sexy or fun or interesting. You want boring sex. Boring I'm just trying to procreate sex. But we are not trying to have children, Parker, so now what?"

"We've been through this. I'm not going to disrespect God because you want sex a certain kind of way—that's unnecessary Selah."

"A certain kind of way. *Humph.* I'm not ashamed that I like raunchy sex, Parker. It turns me on and I'm not going to change so you can look proper to God."

He looked down at his Bible.

"Well I guess I'm just going to have to pray about it."

"Wow," Selah said, deflated. "Go pray then, Parker, if that's what you think you need to do. Just remember you used to like good dirty sex. It's one of the reasons you married me, remember?"

"I did like it, Selah. But it wasn't right for me then either."

Selah got up from the loveseat. *Then maybe you made a mistake,* she said to herself as she walked away. Parker read her thoughts through her silence. He would pray for her after she left. Pray like he always prayed for her, like her soul was going straight to hell. He used to *be* her. She remembered, even if he had forgotten.

Chapter Fifteen

Tina Perkins's older brother was a bad ass. Seventeen years old and threatening juvenile hall every weekend of his petty theft life. It wasn't that he wasn't smart or didn't go to school pretty much every day like most teenagers. He would graduate that year, almost one year early according to his birth certificate. He was born in January 1955 and his mother lied by pushing his age up one year so that he would make the district cut off of being five when school started in September 1959.

Tonio was average in English and history, sometimes even below average, but he excelled in mathematics. Math clicked for him. He was soon to graduate from Pacific High School's class of 1972 to graduate with a D in basic twelfth grade English and a B in calculus. Tonio wasn't unintelligent, he was complicated. He liked thrill more than he liked normalcy. Selah would think of him many days in her adult life and realize that they weren't as different as she had thought they were all those years ago. She would think back on what happened in the park that night and wonder if she really remembered it the way it happened or if she had missed some crucial detail that could change the event's imprint in her mind to a positive one. She now realized that she was a hybrid like Tonio. A mish-mosh of monster and deified saint wrapped into a self she could contain only sometimes.

Selah liked Tonio. *Liked him, liked him.* Thirteen-year-old girl like. She wanted to be alone with him, the way that young girls hope to be alone with someone they have no business being around in the first place. Selah liked the possibility of him. Except for the occasional mall or grocery trip, her world expanded less than one mile in circumference from her neighborhood. Tonio traveled. He knew San Bernardino inside out, even parts of Rialto and Riverside. Selah visited Tina's house almost every day after proving to Mama Gene that she had finished all of her homework. Once there, it was Selah's job to convince Tina that her room was way too hot and because her room was upstairs and heat rises, they should go downstairs where it was cooler and the television was on.

If Tonio didn't complete his calc homework in English, Problems of Democracy, or Bachelor Survival, he usually did it in the dining room attached to the first living room. The second living room was Tina's mother's living room along with her kitchen, her dining room, bathroom, and bedroom. Tonio's bedroom was the only room on that side of the house that Tina's mom shared with anyone. Frieda Perkins essentially had her own apartment with her children living next door; the only people welcomed on Frieda's side of the apartment were her lovers and Tonio.

Tonio and the Perkins family lived on the same block as Selah, six front yards down, on the curve of the elm tree–lined street. Frieda, the mother of Anne, Tonio, Tina, Lojoel, Reesie, and Bobby Lynn, had strict house rules because her house was considered the hangout spot. Between the six of her kids and their friends, her front door never closed good before someone opened it to walk in or out. Besides the popularity of her children, Selah suspected the other reason the house was so popular was because it was the closest thing most of the kids in her neighborhood had ever gotten to a mansion. The Perkinses' apartment was one of only two in Waterman Gardens that had been redesigned to accommodate larger families. The walls between two units had been knocked out and both units had four bedrooms, two kitchens, two living rooms, two dining rooms, and two bathrooms.

There was a vast difference in the two apartments. The kid's side was basic. Couch, loveseat, coffee table, television. Dinette table, four chairs. Mismatched towels, soap, shampoo. Bed, dresser, blanket, cut square of carpet. There was nothing *extra* in their environment. No framed art on the walls or colorful knit throw across the back of the couch. There was no special napkin holder or salt and pepper shakers on the dining table. The things the kids had in the apartment accentuated the things they didn't have. They didn't have the touch of love that made the most run-down ghetto apartment a home.

Mrs. Perkins's side didn't have love either. Her décor had been so meticulously orchestrated that any love she had had been lost somewhere between the crushed red velvet couches covered in yearly updated plastic and the orange matching shag towels that complemented the burnt orange pinstripes on her bathroom wallpaper. The first time Mama Gene visited Frieda's apartment, she could not believe her eyes. Hell-red coated furniture. Mama Gene called it *fifties old-folk plastic.* She believed that there was enough delayed satisfaction in her life without the self-imposed prison of her skin not being able to touch the fabric she'd scraped up pennies to pay for. "I'll be damned," Mama Gene said walking from Frieda's house with Selah's three-year-old hand in hers. "Jesus strike me dead if I ever put some yellowing Saran wrap over my furniture to preserve it for someone else to use after I'm gone. When I'm gone, I'm gone. And looking down from heaven on some ugly, cheap red furniture ain't gone make me feel a bit better."

But Mrs. Perkins's plastic covers never yellowed or gained a tinge of brown in the fitted corners. They never cracked or got sweated on by bare summertime legs. She looked forward to getting the forty percent discount for trading them in each year and getting new ones. Reality was, Mrs. Perkins cared about that plastic as much as she cared about her couches or the red and yellow feather tree with thin plastic wisps exploding from its center or the gold topped floating lamps hanging like three staggered glass rubies from her ceiling.

All of the kids resented the care she put into her half of their apartment. Any one of them would have loved to have been brushed and wiped down and shined the way she did the smoked glass in her six-seat dining table. They would have loved to have been shown and talked about like she showed and talked about the old china she had gotten at a thrift store on Baseline down the street from Bob's Big Boy. They would have loved for her to pour money and attention into them that way, especially Anne. She would never forgive her mother for giving Tonio his own room on her side of the apartment because he was her oldest boy. She was the oldest. She was the one who baby-sat and cooked macaroni and cheese from a box and boiled hotdogs for the family most nights. She was responsible, not Tonio. She deserved her own space, her own four walls without her little sister's friends invading her privacy and sitting on her bed when she wasn't around. She would never forgive her mother for giving her the responsibility of motherhood before her time.

As soon as Selah and Tina galloped downstairs, Anne headed up.

They sat on the stained green flat-cushioned couch. Selah watched Reesie and Bobby Lynn eat the overcooked hotdogs with white bread they had both soaked pink in ketchup. Tonio should be sitting there right now, Selah thought. Reesie and Bobby Lynn wouldn't be playing in ketchup if Tonio were home. The two boys loved Tonio, but more than anything they respected the ever-present possibility that he could whip their bottoms with his bare hands.

Tina and Selah pretended not to be chewing. They had to sneak the brittle brown candy into their mouths small piece by piece to prevent Bobby and Reesie from begging. Selah ate the remaining half of her Chico Stick while watching *Good Times* and analyzing JJ's stick-of-dynamite–thin arms. Tonio should play JJ, Selah thought. He had a quiet charisma that JJ's big ole mouth couldn't even think of capturing. Selah noticed it in the way Tonio ate fruit. Watching him eat an orange was the best. Selah yawned, turning her face toward the back door so that she could expel a reminiscent smile without Tina seeing her do it. She liked the way he leaned back in his chair and smacked as he ate. His fingers molded into the peeled white veined flesh as he sunk his front teeth in deeper. Smack. The juice looked so sweet, moist on his fingers that way. Selah had to eat at least one orange after watching him or even thinking about him eating one. "What," Mama Gene used to say watching Selah hound down her oranges, "have you gone to the Perkins house and caught scurvy eating my oranges like that?" Mama Gene couldn't understand. No one could possibly understand what it would mean to Selah to be ravished that way.

The television blacked out as Tonio's running feet pulled the cord from the wall.

"Cut the fucking lights off," Tonio said, the boxed tape player under his arm falling to the floor, his body falling to the floor behind it. Richard slid over to the couch with a bundle of clothing in his arms.

Selah's Bed

"Turn off the damn lights, Tina."

Nothing else had to be said. Within moments Tina had turned off all the ceiling lights in the kitchen, dining area, and living room. Anne rushed down the stairs to close all the windows and pull the shades. Tina locked the front and back doors. The drill was on. Everyone got down to the floor, Anne, Reesie, Bobby Lynn, Tina, and Selah. They lay with their hearts beating fast against the warm linoleum, legs, arms, and feet overlapping one another's. Footsteps hit the cement porch. They could see an orb from a flashlight appear on one of the pulled shades. The light bounced around and then another light appeared. Everyone lay there, no one moved or spoke. The lights bounced around to several windows, then faded. This was a waiting game; maybe they had moved on to other apartments or maybe they hadn't.

Praise God it was just Kmart security and not the police. Hours later, after the whole ordeal had worn down, Anne socked Tonio in his left arm and socked him again before hugging her head to his chest.

"You know better, Anthony. You're not even supposed to go in the Kmart parking lot anymore, more less the store. You and Richard haven't caught on yet?"

"Didn't nothing happen. Look, we're standing right here," Tonio said.

She took her face from his chest and made a deep wrinkle in her forehead.

"Your stupid ass was lying on the dirty floor just a minute ago, that don't mean nothing to you?"

"SHHHH." He waved both hands in front of his chest. Richard sat with his head against the wall, the two shirts and a pair of black jeans still bundled in his lap.

"You can't go in Kmart yourself, so why are you talking about me?" Tonio said.

"And I *don't go,* Anthony, not unless Momma asks me to and I make sure I never look like I did the day that they caught me."

"It was just an eight track player."

"You're stupid." She fought the urge to slap him on the head. "You know they were going to press charges this time, right? You know Momma wasn't going to come bail you out either, right? She heard all the noise. She hasn't budged out of her room yet, Tonio—that should tell you something." Anne nodded her head yes as if confirming for herself what she already knew. "I'm done with you, man. I'm going back upstairs." She yelled down from the stairs before she turned the hall toward her room. "Richard, you're a stupid ass, too."

"Man, I ain't listening to her," Tonio glanced at Richard, then plopped himself on the couch. "I got homework to do anyway."

No one said anything as Tonio sat with his head resting on the back of the couch, dusting dirt from his dark blue jeans.

"They fucked my shit up," he said, putting three fingers through the hole in the kneecap.

Selah and Tina stayed sitting on the floor. Reesie and Bobby Lynn stayed in their freeze positions and fell asleep under the dining table. Lojoel hadn't made it home yet from his own separate trip to Kmart where he bought himself some Gillette deodorant and a jar of Dixie Peach Pomade. Selah was glad it was Friday. Her curfew wasn't strict on Fridays and Saturdays. She would get home later than normal tonight. Richard would leave at the same time and walk on the opposite side of the street with his new clothes in a brown paper Stater Bros. bag. She would never tell Mama Gene who the flashlights were for; even if Mama Gene found out on her own, Selah wouldn't tell her. She had shared a fear with Tonio that she had never shared with anyone else. And she would take that numbness with her and remember it, every time the television cut off unexpectedly.

Chapter Sixteen

Selah knocked lightly on Parker's study door then pushed it partially open with her fingertips.

"Hey," she said, wedged between the door and its frame.

Parker wiped both of his eyes with his fists. "You can come in. I'm finishing up the lesson for my Sunday school class."

"That's all right," Selah spoke softly, still holding onto the door's outer knob. "I just wanted to see if you'd like some of the jambalaya on the stove before I put the pot in the refrigerator. I just ate some; - it's still warm."

"You can put it in the frig; I'll grab a bowl if I'm hungry later."

Selah flicked the knob. "I can fix you a bowl right quick."

Parker half smiled; his eyes looked sad. "I can get it. Just go on up-stairs; don't worry about me."

Selah inhaled through her nose and paused for a long moment. "You coming to bed soon?" She met his eyes.

"I don't know how long this is going to take."

She let go of the knob. "I'll wait."

Selah was not supposed to remember that Parker used to like for her to graze with her teeth just slightly when she sucked his penis dry of its scent. She should have done herself a favor and forgotten which crevices to place her fingers in and how to scoop her hand around his scrotum sack and squeeze just hard enough so that pain and pleasure confused themselves and became the same thing. She should have.

In moments like this, when she had been waiting in bed for Parker until nighttime switched to wee morning, she remembered most. Selah adjusted her breasts in the see-through white net halter of her derriere-length negligé. She'd tied the front ribbon tight on her chest so that her breasts looked ripe and heavy like tanned guava fruit.

"He wouldn't do this to me again," she said under her breath. Each extra moment of waiting caused her vaginal juices to flow back-ward. Back. Back into walls that would save their moisture for a man who wanted it. Parker would not make her feel dirty for wanting to recapture the peace of his touch. He would not sleep on his office couch and punish her for wanting her shine back and all of her beauty. She could still be the most beautiful woman in Waterman Gardens if he would just let her be.

This is how he hurt her most. When he denied her of the only gift she had that had belonged to him first. Selah had let Tonio take her virginity. She had let neighborhood boys cop feels and put fingers in a place that smelled nothing like candy. But she gave herself to Parker. She gave from an abundant place where thieves and takers - couldn't get to. In exchange for her giving, Parker made her feel beautiful. Sheilia Lester, Tina, and Tasha-Marie had nothing on Selah. Those girls gave her respect and wanted the pride she wore like an amethyst in her eyes. Parker had given this to her. He liked the musk smell under her arms and between her legs. There was nothing dirty about Selah when she was with him. They could put their fingers anywhere. Lick smells and tastes from each other and never have to brush their teeth to suck and lick again.

Michelle changed all of that. They had been together for seven months before Selah got pregnant. But teenage months accrue faster than dog years—doing homework together, talking, making big purple hickeys on each other's necks and trying to freeze them off with the backs of spoons. Selah and Parker had spent several lifetimes and they were happy in the newness of loving.

That morning as she sat in front of her bedroom dresser, putting wood beads and tinfoil tips on the ends of her braids, she decided she would tell him. Selah smiled at herself nervously in the mirror. The hair oil around her face and down the brown lines of her scalp shimmered in the light. There was a brightness in her eyes. She was glad she had braided her hair into ten cornrows that started at the crown of her head and worked themselves down to her nape. She looked different. More mature and full faced with her hair back like that. She stared at herself again. This time standing up and concentrating on the mild shape of her belly. She had known for weeks. So had Mama Gene. But anything that Mama Gene couldn't find out by asking outright, she would find out by conducting research.

For almost three weeks, Mama Gene had followed Selah around. Taking inventory of everything she ate. Checking the bathroom trash can every time Selah closed the door for more than five minutes. At first she didn't know what her grandmother was looking for, but it was clear she was looking for something. When Selah sat on the toilet one night and saw that the seven-layer jawbreaker she had wrapped in toilet tissue and thrown away was unwrapped, she knew what it was. Mama Gene was looking for blood.

Selah had always followed the same menstruation rituals Mama Gene had taught her as an eleven year old. Wearing thick white underwear with a wide crotch. Rolling the used pad into itself as tightly as possible so that the toilet paper wrapped around it would stick. "And wrap it good too," Mama Gene used to say. "I don't want to look down into the trash can as I brush my teeth and see none of your cycle staring back at me." Selah had followed this process to the tee. She rarely had incidents that bled into her clothing and she always had an extra pad in a twist-tie baggie at the bottom of her purse. But no nothing was coming this time.

The next morning when Selah stood at the stove with the refrigerator door opened behind her as she made oatmeal with a swirl of grape jelly and butter mixed in, Mama Gene walked into the kitchen in her housecoat. Instead of reaching inside the cabinet for Folgers, she pulled out a bottle of apple cider vinegar.

"Drink a gulp of this," Mama Gene said, handing Selah the glass bottle.

"Nuh uh, Mama Gene," Selah said. "That's gonna mess up my stomach. I'm about to eat."

Mama Gene didn't flinch. She didn't bat her eyes or fix her mouth to say anything consoling.

"Your stomach's already messed up, and back talking might mess up your mouth."

Mama Gene stood there watching the clear tan liquid flow from the bottle into Selah's mouth. The heaving started deep in Selah's abdomen. She placed both hands over her bulging mouth and crossed over to the sink.

"Why you do that?" Selah said, her face still bent into the basin. She turned the cold water on, ran it over her lips, then gargled. "I'ma have to put my makeup back on now, shoot." Selah crossed her arms under her chest and frowned up her forehead.

Mama Gene stood like a mountain between Selah and the doorway.

"Why do you think you threw up?"

Selah wiped her hands over the imaginary dregs of water still on her face.

"Because it stinks." Selah rolled her eyes and looked to the right of her grandmother's face.

Mama Gene wanted to slap her. Selah knew because she felt an involuntary twinge in her cheek.

Mama Gene slammed her hand down on the counter. "Gurrrl, don't have me hurt you this mornin'. You know as well as I do that you're knocked up. Cut the fire out from under that oatmeal."

Selah reached out her hand to turn the knob, but Mama Gene knocked her hand away and turned it off herself. Selah backed up against the counter.

"I was gonna tell you," she said with her eyes cast down and her voice low.

"You was gonna tell me, hunh? When? When I had to put you in Papa Frank's truck and carry you to the hospital?"

Selah continued looking down. She noticed an old pink Fruit Loop under the edge of the cabinet.

"I was gonna tell you soon, but I wanted to tell Parker first."

"You and your damned momma, boy. I don't know what I did wrong with y'all. How far along are you?"

"I'm five weeks late."

"You took a test?"

"No, I didn't have to."

Mama Gene shook her head a few good times before turning to place the butter and jelly back into the refrigerator. She held the door open for a long time.

"So that boy is gonna take care of this baby?" she finally said, bend-

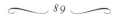

ing to pull a side of salt pork then two bushels of collard greens from the bottom crisper.

Selah scratched a tightly braided spot on the side of her head. "I - ain't told him yet, but I'm gonna tell him after track practice today. Parker is a good man, Mama Gene, he'll do right by me."

Mama Gene snapped. "He ain't no man; he's a boy. A dumb boy who wanted some merry juice from between a stupid girl's legs and got her pregnant."

Selah felt her lip start to shake.

"Now go on and get out of my face," she waved her hand behind her head. "And I'm telling you this, if that boy ain't willing to marry you in the next couple weeks and move you into his parents' house, you ain't keeping that baby. I've done worked too hard."

Selah didn't eat her oatmeal. She didn't grab her books off of the kitchen counter either. When she left the house that day all she had was the bus pass in her pocket. Before talking to Mama Gene, Selah thought Parker might be excited about the baby, but now she wasn't sure.

She sat under the bleachers for the entirety of Parker's practice. She didn't know what to feel, and every time she started to smile it occurred to her to cry. She hadn't planned it. She had always looked at young mothers in her neighborhood with disdain because she knew that fifteen and sixteen was just too young. But Selah wasn't sixteen. She had just turned nineteen and she would be twenty a few months after the baby was born.

She sat there watching Parker's teammates run past through the structure of metal and wood. She had nothing to worry about, she convinced herself. Besides, they were going to do this eventually anyway. They had already decided on moving to Riverside and how many children they were going to have. This was just earlier than expected, that's all.

Parker didn't look surprised when she told him; he looked disappointed. Selah sat atop his letterman jacket and Parker dug his cleats into the dirt.

"I'm not ready. I'm not done with school yet, Selah," is all he said.

Selah grabbed one of the tinfoil tips of her braids and looked up into the stands so not to cry.

"What do you mean, you're not done with school? I'm pregnant now."

Parker shrugged his shoulders. "I'm just not done with school, - that's all."

This was the farthest away from her Parker had ever sat in all of the time they had been dating. He had always been kissing her neck or rubbing the inside of her thigh trying to coax her juices. But sitting under the bleachers today he was quiet and doe-eyed, answering questions respectfully so that he could be dismissed.

Selah didn't know where the man she had been making love to all these months had gone. All she saw now was a scared little boy, and all she heard was Mama Gene's words. *If that boy don't marry you, you ain't keeping that baby.* Selah pulled her knees to her chest and tried not to give way to the nervousness tingling under her skin.

"So what does this mean?" she said, careful not to look Parker in the eyes.

"Well, for me it means that I still have another semester to do here at the JC before I transfer to a four-year. I may go out of state; maybe grad school. I'm not sure."

Selah shook her head. "So what you're saying is that this baby is my responsibility and school is yours, huh? Is that what you are trying to tell me?"

Parker just looked at Selah.

"Ugghh." She kicked the dirt in front of her. "*You* the one that - didn't want to use condoms *no* more," she punctuated her words with low dips in her voice. "*You* the one who said that *pre-come* don't have *enough power* and that you would pull out before you *e-jac-u-late. Nig-gah please.*"

Parker waved his hands in front of his face. "Man, I gotta think about this. You can't just spring this on me and expect me to—"

"It got sprung on me; what am I supposed to do?"

His look was blank. Selah kicked the dirt again.

Selah was angry with herself. Angry for forgetting what Tina had looked her in the eyes and told her years ago: *Never let a boy go in you bare, especially if you love him.* Tina hadn't said the *especially* part, but Selah updated Tina's thirteen-year-old wisdom to include something Tina had probably figured out for herself already.

Chapter Seventeen

Tonio invited her to see *Come Back, Charleston Blue*. It was coming to the Crest Theater on E Street, walking distance from the Ritz and the California Theater, which would become the Pussy Cat Theater less than five years from the day he asked her. He hadn't asked her on a date per se. It was more of a why don't you come along kind of thing. "A bunch of us are riding out to the Crest Saturday night for *Charleston Blue;* you and your *homies* can come." She knew he liked her then. Tonio loved his younger sister, would kick someone's behind if they messed with Tina, but he never invited her to hang with him and his friends.

So that day when Tonio turned the corner from Crest View to Sycamore, walking with a cool lean, dipping with each right step, left arm hanging at his side, his right arm scooping the air behind him with each dip, Selah froze. He had on doo-doo brown corduroy pants that hugged his thighs then flared below the knee and a brown, white, and beige polyester button-down shirt with a flap collar. His fro was short and packed tight.

All Selah had been doing anyway was getting some fresh air. Mama Gene refused to turn the air conditioning back on that afternoon because she said it was almost five o'clock and the breeze from the opened windows and the screen doors should be enough to keep cool till the sun went down. Mama Gene had lost her damned mind. It was hot. The type of day that got hotter and more oppressive as evening approached, bringing its early summer humidity with it. Selah lay in her bed atop her sheets, with the square metal window fan angled toward her face. The breeze felt desert on her skin. She tried to lie still. When she wiped her hand across her neck, a thin gray line of dead skin and grime collected. She rolled the skin under her thirteen-year-old fingers. She flicked her nails. She opened and closed her thighs listening to the smacking sound they made as they suctioned apart. When she finally couldn't take the walled-in heat any longer, the sheets stuck to the back of her legs when she got up.

Selah sat on the pink two-foot-high cement wall that enclosed part of the walkway leading to her front door. Her legs straddled either side of its foot-long width. She leaned back and stretched her arms over her head. The overhang of the roof cast just enough shadow so that sun hit half of her body at a diagonal, but not her eyes. It was cooler outside than it was in the house, she thought. Normally Selah was cautious about what she wore outside, even if she was only going across the street to take Miss Dottie the three eggs and cup of flour she had called Mama Gene to borrow. Even at thirteen, some types of clothing could already look awkward on her or make her look more woman than she really was. Selah adjusted the baby blue shorts with plastic waist band and white line going up the sides. She pulled the white tube top well over her chest so that neither of her breasts hung out on the sides as she lay down. She was starting to feel good, and that's when she noticed Tonio walking toward her on her side of the street.

Selah's Bed

Hammer bitch, she thought to herself. She lazily flopped her arms over her eyes, trying to make the action look natural, like she hadn't seen him coming.

When Tonio stood perpendicular to Selah's body he stopped and placed his white Converse on the curb.

"You didn't go down to the swimming pool with Tina and them?"

She shook her head no coolly, her arms moving from over her eyes to her forehead.

"What, your grandma don't like you catching the bus that far?" Tonio kept his foot on the curb and took the fisted afro pick from the middle of his head and placed it back.

"Highland ain't that far."

"For a twelve year old it might be."

Tonio was seventeen and he knew that Selah wasn't twelve because he had eaten a piece of her birthday cake that past year and had gotten the slice with the three on top of it.

"I'm thirteen, and if your sister is old enough to go by herself without your momma, so am I."

"Unh, unh," he shook his head and smiled, curling his tongue behind his front teeth. "Yo grandma's, different, you're one of them streetlight kids. She ain't gonna let you far enough away from her for you to piss crooked."

"Your momma is the one with the plastic on her furniture," she smiled and raised her arms over her head to punctuate her statement.

Tonio lowered his head, smiling, then smoothed his chin with his right hand. "True-that. But my momma uptight about her furniture—her kids are something different." He kept smiling. "And - that's why your little ass is here while all your homies are swimming and hooping it up. A half day of school on a Friday? In summer? Shit, yo grandma got you whooped." Tonio said the last part low, almost mouthing it in case Mama Gene was in listening distance.

"You didn't go." Selah came back quick.

Tonio smiled bigger, almost mischievously. "I had some business to take care of. Some grown-up business." He laughed and covered his mouth with his fist, surprised by how loudly he laughed but proud and tickled with his answer.

"Anyways," Selah said, at a loss for words, hoping that her rolled eyes gave balance to her awkwardness.

Tonio took his foot off of the curb. "Well I'm gonna check you later. If you feel like it, a few of us are going to ride out to see *Charleston Blue* tomorrow if you and your silly friends want to roll."

Selah just shook her head and placed her arms back over her eyes. She wanted to jump out of her skin. She turned her face toward the screen door and smiled with full teeth as Tonio walked away. She - couldn't wait for her friends to get back from swimming; she would tell them everything.

Chapter Eighteen

March 11, 1978

Sometimes when I write, I try to make me different. I try to become something other than I am. I am a nineteen-year-old mother-to-be. I do not feel you turning in my stomach, but I know you are here. There is a wound knot in the center of me that tightens every time I cry. This must be you. You are only weeks old in my womb. My blood has stopped flowing and I am cradling you in the lining of my flesh. I have never had eyes on the inside of me besides my own. I see more clearly because of you.

I must tell you this. And though my words whisper, you must hear the ringing in their timbre: You will have to fight to be here. I have been told that babies hear voices from the outside. That's why I never scream or listen to loud music anymore. And if you can hear, that means you can feel. So when Parker and Mama Gene try to wrap their hands around my stomach, don't let them in. Don't let their energy change what you know about me. I am your mother. They will not poison you. You will not think that you ruined anything because you exist. I want you. I have never felt anything grand before you. And I write you these letters as my pact. I will love you always. When you are older, these letters will be your record. Of how things were. Of how things should have been.

Chapter Nineteen

Riding out meant everyone meeting at the Perkins house around twelve o'clock that afternoon and walking posse-deep into downtown San Bernardino with enough time left to catch a bite at Pail O' Chicken or Mickey D's, then secure a good spot in the movie theater with a tub of hot buttered popcorn. This process usually took four to five hours. It was a casual process. The kind of thing you eased into without rush or hurry, like good sex.

Tina, Tasha-Marie, and Carla couldn't believe it when Selah told them they were invited to hang with the high schoolers that weekend.

"You're moded, corroded, your booty exploded," Tasha-Marie said with scathing attitude, sitting on the orange shag rug at the end of Tina's bed. "Plain busted."

"Swear," Tina chimed in excitedly from the edge of the bed, her bare feet striking the floor with rapid succession causing Tasha-Marie's head to move up and down with each jolt.

"I swear," Selah said.

"On a stack of Bibles," Tina said, upping the ante.

"You either trust me or you don't," Selah said dismissively and adultlike, meeting Tina's red, chlorine flushed eyes. Tina jumped up and down harder, the pink tube of lipstick on her bed moving toward the edge. The group let out a collective *Whew*. Selah smiled.

Carla sat in the beanbag under the opened window, her small fragile frame enveloped on both sides by red pleather. "Mama Gene gonna let you come?" she said distractedly, as she concentrated on pulling the soft, clear nail off of her waterlogged thumb.

Selah jumped from Indian-style onto her knees. She spoke fast. "I already explained it. I asked Mama Gene if I could spend the night here tomorrow and if she could give me five dollars in case Anne and Tonio decided to take us to the afternoon movie with them on Saturday. And you guys know how much Mama Gene loves Anne and how she used to let her baby-sit me when I was little. That was it. Oh, I also told her that your mother," she looked at Tina, "said that it was all right for me to stay over."

"So she just said yeah?" Tina asked.

Selah plopped back down on her butt and pulled her legs into her body by her toes. "She felt bad about not letting me go swimming with you guys and making me sit in the hot house by myself until you guys got back."

"So, is this a *date?*" Tasha-Marie asked, her face seasoned with non-expression. "You and Tonio hooking up?"

Selah shrugged her shoulders. She didn't know what it was. All she knew was that she would get over to Tina's house early on Saturday to borrow one of Tina's blouses to match her blue bells. Since Tina was about three sizes smaller than Selah, Tina's clothes always made Selah's chest look bigger and Mama Gene would never buy Selah anything that she thought was too small.

"Would you do him?" Carla asked.

Selah flicked her wrist at her. "You are nasss-ty. Why's your mind in the gutter—Would you?"

Carla put the torn thumbnail into her mouth and mumbled. "If he was my man fo' real, I might would."

Everybody giggled; the excitement of experiencing the possibility of lust was the only thing they understood about romantic love.

"Would you let him touch you?" Carla leaned in toward Selah. Tasha-Marie and Tina waited for an answer as well.

Selah wouldn't answer them. Not for real anyway. She had let several boys feel her up. Flesh feels, basketball and playground dirty hands under the tight elastic of a training bra she had outgrown. The right boy could put his hands on the outside of her pant-covered crotch and feel the pelvic bones that surrounded a soft middle that sunk in with touch.

"I think *you* want him," Selah said, switching up the deck. "I see the way you watch him eating fruit, like you wish it was your snatch in his mouth."

"Na, uh. You lyin'," Carla's voice was high-pitched and strong. "I think *Lojoel* is cute. Tonio's breath stinks when he gets too close, like maybe he's been eating out the wrong na-na."

They laughed again. Selah watched Tina throw up the Winnie the Pooh bear Anne had given her from her grad night two years ago for not telling their mother that she and Renee Lester got kicked out of Kmart for stealing and weren't allowed back into the store.

Selah stared at Tina as the girls went on talking about Carla liking Lojoel and Lojoel only being eleven years old. Selah nodded and smiled mimicking their actions so to seem a part of the conversation. Selah wondered if Tonio *did* have a girlfriend. If he did bring girls up to his dark, sneaker-smelling room to grind them on his bed to loudly playing Parliament when he thought no one else was home. She'd never seen him with anyone before. Sometimes he played around with the girls in the Gardens, wore their thin gold chains around his neck and stuff, but nothing serious. Selah remembered sitting on the back porch with Tina when they were around ten as Tonio played Hide and Go Get It with the rest of the kids on the block his age. But everyone did that at some point in their lives. Even Selah and her friends had graduated from Cooties and tapping out on the curb to hiding and getting.

Tonio could have a Mexican girlfriend, Selah thought. He was always hanging out with Richard Frijo. Richard was a pale-skinned Mexican guy with slick black hair and the slightest bit of fuzz on his chin that never grew in enough to connect with his long sideburns to form a beard. Richard was an honorary black guy as far as Tonio was concerned, and Richard called Tonio an honorary Mexican. He and Tonio walked the Waterman Gardens streets together so often, no one thought anything when they saw Richard by himself strolling with his Chicano pimp daddy lean down Elm or Sycamore. Tonio and Richard were tight, blood brothers even. That's how Tonio came to be called Tonio instead of Anthony Rayvon and why Richard walked around with a black fisted afro pick in his right rear pocket.

"He's almost *twelve*," Carla said, her voice even higher this time, frail and long like her body. "By the time we are in high school, he will be a junior and I will be a senior. Then when we graduate, it - won't even matter."

Maybe it was Richard's sister Tonio dated. Selah knew Richard had a younger sister named Carolina because her name was tattooed on his left arm in flagrant green cursive letters with flourishes on the C, R, L, and A. It could be Richard's sister or even some chick he met in Richard's neighborhood or a neighboring high school like Cajun or Eisenhower. Richard lived a few blocks east of Mount Vernon on Congress Street and Selah knew nothing about that world or anyone in it besides Richard. Selah pulled her legs in closer to her body. She would be an outsider for the rest of the evening. Her butt would ache as she sat in the same stale position on Tina and Anne's hard, speckled bedroom floor. She would smell the clean chlorine smell emanating from the three wet swimsuits spread out on a towel in the walkway between Tina's half-made bed and the long mirrored dresser against the wall. She would see Carla reach into the back of the torn beanbag and throw two handfuls of puffy white dots at Tasha-Marie and Tina for saying that she was trying to *do-the-do* to an eleven-year-old, still in the sixth grade. Selah would be a part of all of these things, but not really. She was thinking about Tonio, Anthony Rayvon Perkins, and how he was the reason she ate a peeled sectioned orange every night before sleeping.

Chapter Twenty

Selah took another lover today. Not physically, but in her heart. It was one of those unexpected happenings. Like finding a forgotten twenty-dollar bill in the small square pocket of her jeans. He was like that. Familiar. Pepper and a dash of salt around his hairline. Mustache enough to graze her bottom lip when they spoke close, leaving a lingering tingle below the surface. He was raw heat distilled by the art of loving well and she knew it.

Selah watched as he took the stainless-steel ladle in his hand and poured a single helping of vegetarian chili into a thick porcelain bowl. She smiled behind her eyes. A man who could control himself in a buffet-style setting was impressive. Reminded her of Parker after he accepted God into his life.

The man placed the bowl and two packets of oyster crackers next to the small salad on his tray and began to look for a seat. She wanted him. Not in the way a person wants an ice-cold Coke or slice of double chocolate cake, but the way you want water when saliva feels like dust in your throat. As he scanned the lunchtime crowd, it occurred to Selah to offer him the empty seat next to her. But a part of her wanted to long for him. Wonder what he smelled like, what his voice sounded like, if his stare would make her feel nude or safe. They locked eyes for a full moment. Selah looked away knowing she didn't have to. She pretended to ignore the warm air his strut generated as he passed her.

She wanted to shoot him slow shutter, .35 millimeter, black and white. Talk him into relaxed poses only his momma and best lover could get him into. He would start out as he looked now. Pull off his tie-on-top Stacy Adams shoes and silk socks ribbed lengthwise. Selah would sit Indian-style on the studio floor in front of him, capturing the laughter in his cheekbones, the anxiety in his shoulders from being seen by a woman as truly beautiful. She would find her childhood in him. The moments before adulteration and absences were realized. And like she did with every man she invited into her private spaces, from behind the camera, she would look for pieces of a man she used to know. She'd never had a father; Parker was the only man she'd known well enough to ever miss.

The only item left on her tray that she hadn't touched was the gelatin. She sliced her fork through the wobbly strawberry cube and sucked its chilled redness into her mouth. She believed in eating everything on her plate; she was raised that way. Having to sit at Mama Gene's table for hours until her butt was flat and all the stewed tomatoes and okra were gone. Her grandmother's pork chops fried in bacon grease still stuck to her thighs. She liked it though, the fullness of being what she called a "true" voluptuous woman. Not large, but built with just enough jelly to keep herself and someone else comfortably warm.

She would keep him warm. Not today, but another evening, after he'd let her shoot him nude and he'd figured out that she loved with her whole self at first kiss.

Chapter Twenty-One

Selah took the front street to Tina's house that morning. She usually took the back way, through the grass, but this Saturday morning she didn't want to have wet blades of grass sticking to her toes or to the leather of her new white sandals. The sandals weren't new because she'd just bought them; they were new because she never wore them when she played double dutch or scuffed them when she sat outside talking on the Gate. These were her *got it going on* sandals. The ones like Ruthie Mae wore the time she took Selah to McDonald's in her sparkly short-shorts. Selah even tried to walk like Ruthie Mae when she wore them. She extended her hips more to one side than the other so that her sway had a curvy, rhythmic appeal. Selah remembered how all the men stared at Ruthie that day. She remembered Ruthie Mae becoming strong with each witnessed stride. Ruthie Mae took those looks home with her that night. She bottled them and took them out on days off when she lay around her small, damp apartment. Selah had learned from her mother that that kind of attention could make you resilient. And Selah never worried about Ruthie Mae because she knew the dampness of her small world would never settle into her.

Selah walked with her travel case slung over her shoulder, practicing the technical aspects of her walk—where she placed her hands, the distance of each step. When she arrived on the Perkinses' doorstep it was a few minutes before ten. She could tell that Carla and Tasha-Marie were already there because she heard giggles come from Tina's open room window followed by a hard silence.

"This ain't just your room, Tina, and I don't get any privacy with your friends coming over here all the time. Don't your friends have houses, too? Why don't y'all go hang at Mama Gene's house sometimes?"

"We're just going to the movies with Tonio and them today and—"

"What about yesterday?"

"We went swimming."

"And the day before that?"

Selah didn't hear a reply.

"Exactly," Anne said. "Go over to their houses sometimes and let me have our room to myself."

Selah never had to knock when she walked into the Perkins house, but she felt like knocking this time. The travel case on her shoulder made her feel even more invasive. She opened the screen door, passed the narrow kitchen that was just like Mama Gene's, then the raggedy dinette set. Selah intercepted Anne as she emerged from the stairwell with her bedding jumbled in her arms. Selah would normally say hello, but she didn't this time. Anne rolled her eyes and plopped her stuff on the couch.

"Go on up," she said, flipping the television on. Selah walked up the stairs quietly, trying not to have one piece of wood squeak as she walked. They must have woken Anne up, Selah thought. Anne's hair was uncombed and she still had her pajamas on.

"Hey, hey, hey, it's F-A-A-A-A-T ALBERT," trailed up the stairs behind Selah. And as Selah walked into Tina's room and got congratulated on how good her hair looked, Anne sat balled up on the couch knowing that she'd be a damned fool to walk to the movies that afternoon with a bunch of high schoolers and four kids. Going anywhere meant freedom for Tonio, regardless of whom he was with. All Tonio really had to do around the house was wipe his behind and Frieda Perkins was satisfied with that. Anne going anywhere in the company of Selah, Tina, Tasha-Marie, and Carla meant baby-sitting. Anne knew that she would fare far better staying her responsible tail at home. Lojoel would be playing outside all day and just coming in every so often to sneak a drink of Kool-Aid directly from the pitcher or a swig of water from the faucet if someone was around. Reesie and Bobby Lynn would be picked up by their biological father's mother.

Anne leaned forward from the couch to turn up the volume and to adjust the round knobs on the back of the television that controlled horizontal hold. She was tired of always being the one in charge. Her mother never gave her credit for doing anything right and the only money she made was from baby-sitting children other than her siblings. Mama Gene was the only person who had ever paid her really good anyway. Five dollars for five hours or ten dollars for anything past eight. But Selah was big now, thirteen and pretty much a bad ass like - Anne's little sister Tina. Anne hated the way the four of them would bounce into the room and take over like she wasn't there. She was too nice and she only had two steadfast rules that she'd bite their heads off over: They had to stay off of her bed and out of her clothes and makeup.

As long as they did those things, she was basically cool with them, except for when they woke her up. Anne was the oldest child in the Perkins family and the first girl so she understood firsthand how important it was for younger girls to have someone to look up to. She would be that for them—she'd even occasionally style their hair in a flip and fix them up in makeup. Anne wrapped her arms tight around her stomach, knowing that to have her own baby was different from pampering her younger sister and her friends. Maybe this was her way out.

"Your grandma did your hair?" Tina came over to feel the softness of Selah's press and curls.

"Mama Gene hot combed it and I rolled it myself. But Mama Gene cut my bangs 'cause last time I cut 'um crooked."

"I'ma ask Annie to cut me some tomorrow," Tina added, meaning Selah's bangs looked cute.

Selah sat the hard blue travel case on the floor and let the piece of rope she'd attached as a shoulder strap hang to the side. She was proud of herself. Proud of her hair and her formfitting polyester bell-bottoms with the sewn in, raised crease going down the front. She was proud of her new leather shoes and the blouse she was going to borrow from Tina that would make her outfit complete.

Selah had harassed Mama Gene all night into straightening her hair. Selah sat at Mama Gene's feet while Mama Gene tried to complete the Sunday crossword puzzle from the week before.

"Selah, I've already told you, you better let me alone so I can finish my puzzle. The new one comes out in a couple of days and I don't want to get behind."

Mama Gene did crossword puzzles like they were weekly algebra assignments. She was methodical and thoughtful. She kept a notepad where she'd record possible answers and only when she was positive that the answers were correct did she pencil in the words in clear bubble letters. It was only the *white* words that Mama Gene - wouldn't get. Words like: *What four-letter cheese goes well with a baguette?*

"I know what four-letter word goes well with this puzzle right now; that's what I know. What the hell *is* a baguette, more less some brie? Only cheese choices I know are Kraft or Colby." She laughed.

Selah sat there, being patient, whining *Please* only on occasion and pulling on the hem of Mama Gene's housecoat when she felt completely ignored.

"You have one more time to break my concentration, Selah, and I'm gonna break in your backside over my knee."

"Please, Momma," Selah whined again and threw her head lifelessly on the cushion of the couch.

Mama Gene studied the silence in Selah's eyes.

"Go on in the kitchen then, hurry up. Get the straightening comb, thick comb, and the grease. Quick, or you'll be looking like a little nappy-headed pickaninny tomorrow."

Selah ran off, collected everything Mama Gene needed, and placed them on the counter next to the stove. She softened in a sad way, almost like a wilted flower. Mama Gene never realized that - she'd raise a daughter like Ruthie Mae. Mama Gene always thought that she'd raise a proud woman. But Ruthie Mae wasn't a proud woman; she was an arrogant one. This is what she had given Selah for a mother, and she felt sorry for that every time she heard the word *Momma* pop from Selah's mouth.

"Comb that mess out, Selah, before I get up, 'cause you ain't gonna like it if I have to tear through those be-bes in the back of your head. It darn well better be clean, too. I have told you about half washing your hair. You half wash those dishes the same way."

Mama Gene could have said anything to Selah right then. Selah stood in front of the stove smiling as she pulled every kink from her hair. She was going to look good for Tonio tomorrow.

After Mama Gene was done, Selah dragged a dinette chair by its pyramid-shaped back down the hall and into her bedroom. She placed the vinyl chair so that she would be in the center of the large scalloped mirror attached to her dresser. She would use her new Goodie brand curlers for this job, not the deflated, dingy pink ones under the bathroom sink that Mama Gene used occasionally as well.

Selah watched herself as she wound the beautifully burnt-smelling hair, which she had parted in sections with a fine-toothed comb, around the spongy pink flesh of the curler. Usually she was lazy when she did this. She would talk on the phone with one of her friends as she pulled her fingers through the barely pressed crop of hair on her head creating a zigzag of a part. But the sections tonight would be different. Selah would turn her head into a perfectly lined grid of hair and scalp.

Tonio's crew didn't show up until around twelve thirty, but Selah and her friends were ready by eleven. They moved down to the living room, allowing Anne to go back up to her room and sleep.

Tina wore a powder puff pink overall jumper that would have only covered half of Selah's butt, but because Tina was so short, the hemline stopped closer to her knees. Tasha-Marie, the bad-mamma-jamma, most proportionate one of the crew, wore a T-shirt with a rainbow traveling from her left shoulder to the right side of her flat stomach that matched the rainbow belt looped through her blue jeans. And Carla wore what she always wore anywhere she considered important—a thin floral print dress with a long flimsy belt, which she knotted around her waist.

Selah sat on the couch, careful to keep her back straight so that no rolls appeared around her stomach. She liked the way Tina's button-down paisley blouse made her feel. She was definitely the most womanly of all of them. As the rest of them sat between the couch and the loveseat watching *Soul Train,* Selah would glance down at her breast when she thought no one was looking. Ripe breast, she thought, not little rosebuds like her friends.

"What you bring?" Tina asked Selah, facing her with her left knee squared off on the couch.

"Abba Zabba and lemonheads," Selah said. "What you bringing?"

"You know that Abba Zabba is going to make your lips white," Tasha-Marie said.

"Not if she eats it right," Tina said. "I brought a Big Daddy and a pack of purple Kool-Aid with sugar mixed in."

"I'm taking some Sugar Babies," Tasha-Marie put the box up to her lips and popped two into her mouth.

"Why you quiet, Carla, you didn't bring nothin'?" Tina said.

"Yeah," Carla said, opening the old green purse. "I just brought those pink dots and some orange chews with the sugar sprinkles." She pulled the Stater Bros. plastic produce bag from her purse. - "That's all my momma had in the cabinet and I might want to buy a hamburger or some popcorn at the movie."

"Ain't no thang," Tasha-Marie said, grabbing a chew from Carla's bag. "I hit up my momma and that tired old dog she dates so you can share with me."

When Tonio walked downstairs from the next door apartment, he didn't say anything. He walked past all of them and went directly into the kitchen to pour himself some milk and grab some cookies. The girls looked at Selah after he passed. She shrugged her shoulders. A warm sensation spread through her cheeks. Tonio didn't even look at her. He didn't look at her blouse or how her hair was parted down the middle of her head with thin blue barrettes on either side. He didn't notice her new bangs.

"He better not do this," Tina said under her breath.

"I told you Selah was lying," Tasha-Marie said under her breath.

Tonio wouldn't do something jacked up like that, Selah told herself. He liked her and she knew he did no matter what anyone said. She sat there with her back straight, watching *Soul Train*. She wouldn't allow herself to think about the fact that she was only thirteen and that Tonio was seventeen and about to graduate from high school. She wouldn't allow herself to think about the fact that he completely ignored her as he stood in the kitchen doorway eating Oreos. And when his friends arrived, thirty minutes after Don Cornelius had kissed the airwaves good-bye, she absolutely wouldn't allow herself to think about the light-skinned girl with the pretty lavender scarf wrapped around her full sandy brown afro. Selah wouldn't allow herself to think about any of this, but all of a sudden her blouse felt too small, her hair fried and greasy, and her neck dirty like she hadn't showered the night before.

"Y'all coming or what?" Tonio yelled through the wood-framed screen door back into the house.

Tina, Tasha-Marie, and Carla popped up. Selah managed to eke out half a smile.

The group of nine walked down Baseline, turned north on E Street to hit Pail O' Chicken, ate, then backtracked south to make it to the Crest Theater in time for the five o'clock showing of *Come Back, Charleston Blue*.

"I know Charleston Blue is going to kick some ass in this movie," Tonio said, taking out his dollar twenty-five to pay for his ticket.

"Man, I heard he has a blue steel razor and shit," Richard pulled two dollars from the front pocket of the black jeans he had stolen from Kmart.

"I heard he's a pimp and a pusher though," the lavender scarf girl said.

"Shit, pimps need love too. You gonna give me some?" Tonio said and the rest of the crew laughed except for Selah.

"Anyway, Tonio. Well," she rolled her eyes, "well, as long as every woman in the movie ain't his ho, I can dig it." Lavender girl smiled again. Tina, Tasha-Marie, and Carla smiled too.

They thought she was pretty and that she had a nice butt and cute flower decals on her toenails. Selah thought she was pretty too, but whereas the other girls looked up to her, Selah considered her competition.

Lavender girl was winning. Even Selah was surprised at how gracefully she had walked a couple of miles in those wedge heels and wasn't even limping yet. Selah was limping. It was a controlled, sore right heel and left arch limp. Selah, Tasha-Marie, Tina, and Carla had walked in back of the caravan the entire time so no one could really notice Selah's limp, but no one was paying attention anyway. Everyone was paying attention to *Tammie*. That's how the girls knew that Tammie had a nice butt; they'd been staring at it for the better portion of the afternoon. And Selah was tired. Tired of walking and tired of Tammie's ass.

Prime seating in the Crest Theater was in the balcony. The balcony was considered overfill so unless a movie sold completely out, the group would have the entire area almost completely to themselves. Tonio, Richard, Lavender girl, and the Bowen twins sat in the front row. Tina, Selah, Carla, and Tasha-Marie sat behind them.

Tina made out on the popcorn and root beer because Selah was so excited when Richard sat next to Miss Lavender and not Tonio that she could barely concentrate on the movie or eating. Selah watched Tonio eat. She watched him drink his Coke from a red-and-white striped straw. She even saw a fine line of saliva snap from the straw back to his lip. Selah was so happy in this moment, she thought the evening could only get better from here. And it would get better. And after that, it would get worse.

Chapter Twenty-Two

Mama Gene mixed her pills. She put them into a white aspirin bottle or stripped the information labels off of the brown bottles given
by the pharmacy and funneled them in like confetti. Blue ones,
white ones, pink ones, orange. Papa Frank believed she did this because without the pills being in the correct bottles with the labels on
them, she figured no one would know what she was taking and
which pills were which. She was basically right. It was impossible to
memorize the color, shape, and function of every pill that Mama
Gene took.

She'd taken so many over the years. She started taking them regularly when Ruthie Mae was about twelve, and Selah was now eigh-
teen. Mama Gene had given twenty-one faithful years of service to
the pharmaceutical industry and doctors with free-flowing prescription pads. And there were so many out there—doctors and pills.
Mama Gene spread her symptoms around so that Dr. Pasuak treated
her for her back, Dr. Snowdon for the headaches, Dr. Andersval for

the ligament in her left calf. Mama Gene was faithful to her doctors and they were faithful to her. She never canceled appointments, she always showed up on time, and the doctors made sure that she rarely stayed in their offices for more than fifteen minutes a visit. Sometimes Mama Gene didn't even have to go into an office; she could leave a message the night before with the doctor's answering service and have a prescription waiting for her at the pharmacy the next afternoon.

Mama Gene loved her doctors. Since she was a licensed vocational nurse, she paid attention to the samples various pharmaceutical companies sent to the convalescent hospital where she worked. She skimmed through the *Physicians' Desk Reference* in the back office and updated her nurses' drug guidebook every year. As her immunity to the drugs increased, she often switched to completely new medicines or upped the doses. She knew which pills would make her sleep, take away the pain, and calm her down, so she mixed varying amounts of each to create her perfect insurance-covered high.

Papa Frank knew that none of the pills Mama Gene took were for what he considered real problems. She wasn't on high blood pressure medication and she didn't take anything for heart palpitations or the like. Papa Frank was free and clear in his conscience to throw any pill he came across down the toilet. That's how Mama Gene learned to keep four or five mixed bottles in various parts of the house so that in case Papa Frank found part of her stash, she'd have a backup supply to make it through the evening. But all the stash in the world didn't stop her from cursing the black off his behind every time he did it.

"Mathis you are an ornery cuss," she screamed, marching her full body down the hall toward the living room with a cleaning towel in her hand. "And don't even twist your chapped lips to tell me you -

don't know what the hell I'm talking about. You took my pills, you dirty dog, and I ain't waiting for you to give them back either. Give me my pills. Now, Mathis."

Papa Frank's spot was on the left end of the couch so that he could easily reach down and grab the bottle of Night Train at his side.

Mama Gene walked up to him and towered over his sitting body like a brown mountain.

"Now I don't touch your brown bag so you stop touching my stuff; you're making me look bad. Always having to get refill after refill because you throw my pills away."

"You're making your own self look bad," he said, grabbing his brown bag from the floor and placing it between his legs. Papa Frank knew if he didn't grab his drink quickly, Mama Gene would pour it out if she got ahold of it.

Papa Frank beating her to the bag made her more angry. From the grogginess of her voice and the way her shoulders were tensed up to her ears, he knew she was out. Papa Frank smiled to himself, but only on the inside.

Mama Gene turned off the television. "Get your clodhoppers off my coffee table." She slapped his feet away with her hand, then bent down to clean the boot mark off of the wood.

From the smell of bleach on the towel in her hand, Papa Frank figured she had been cleaning the bathroom when she realized he had taken the pill bottle out of the toilet's water tank; he'd also swiped the three white ones she'd wrapped in clear plastic and put in the almost empty jar of Miracle Whip. Papa Frank was amazed by her versatility.

Mama Gene had duct taped the pill bottle to the inside of the porcelain overflow tank. She'd taped it to the very top with the expectation that the water would never flow that high.

"Way I see it," Papa Frank took a swig of wine, "you didn't factor in the moisture of the tank. Had you factored in the moisture, you might have placed a cup holder over the back of the tank and just placed them in there. You got a smart man, you know that."

She was too through with him, and the aching in her body was causing her to shake. From her nursing background, it looked to her like the beginnings of a heroin shake, the way her hand pulsed back involuntarily.

"Saw that," Papa Frank said, pointing to her hand with his bottle.

Mama Gene marched her way into the kitchen. She slammed the cabinet door closed so hard it bounced open again.

"You just a damned alcoholic anyway," she said.

Papa Frank smiled toward the kitchen, knowing that even if she couldn't see him smiling she could feel it. "Miss clinical specialist," he added a manufactured slur to his voice. "I'm not an ak-ca-holic or a drunk; I'm a wino. Be specific when you call me out my name." He smiled again.

Mama Gene almost laughed; he wanted her to laugh. He sounded absolutely ridiculous to her, but she was too angry.

"And if you would just own up," he continued, "to the fact that you're a mult-tie-fer—mult-tie-fair—mult-tie—Eugenia, what's that word that was on your crossword puzzle last week?"

There was no way in hell she would tell him that word so he could turn around and insult her with it.

With wine bottle in hand, Papa Frank walked down the hall to the bedroom to get the crossword puzzle from the nightstand. He walked back into the living room and took his spot again.

"And if you would just own up," he continued, "to being a mult-tie-fair-ious pill-popper addict, like I did about being a wino, you'd do a whole lot better for yourself."

Mama Gene would grab her purse and be out the front door before Papa Frank would finish detailing what he thought she was and what she needed to do about it. Mama Gene would catch the number 12 bus to find herself a new pharmacy in Rialto or somewhere. She was tired of the pharmacists at Savon, Thrifty's, and Longs Drugs who gave her funny looks when she came in to get her medicine. She was not an addict. *Addict* was a term reserved for street people and illegal drug users like Ruthie Mae and that no-good boyfriend of hers. Mama Gene would never consider herself an addict, no matter what anyone thought she was. She was a patient.

Chapter Twenty-Three

She knew she'd see him again; she'd been waiting. Gently waiting, not stalking like some folks would call it. Selah had always been this way. When she got an idea stuck in her head real tough, she had to follow it all the way through. Tonio was one of the things.

Pepper Dash of Salt was one of those things too. She'd been thinking about him since the moment she smelled the faint mist of his cologne on the air of his strut. Pepper Dash of Salt wasn't studying Selah. His common sense and composure didn't break down under the gentle wobble of thick thighs. She smiled. Selah smiled big, showing the small gap between her front teeth that she never chose to have filled. *Big leg-ged, brown skinned-ed, gap tooth-ed, French kiss your daddy good with all this lovin'* used to be her title for herself in her twenties. In her *I'm old enough for you not to ask my age* stage, she could have sported even a mega gap with style. Something about the way she felt about herself made her know this.

Sometimes a big girl with confidence could be too much for some people. They wanted to quiet her down and put her in her place. - That's why Selah started to get most of her clothing tailored in the first place. If she wanted a split showing all the flava of her thigh, she could have one. If she wanted the deepest valley between her rotund breast to show, she could have that too. If anyone stared too hard or too long at her, she'd often go over to them and give them a whisper: "Big ain't nev-va got betta than this," and walk off bigger than she came. Selah was tasteful though; the good stuff was saved for the bedroom and the bedroom didn't call for clothing, it called for *everything you can see, you can have* confidence. Selah'd learned confidence from her mother. Confidence, in Selah's opinion, wasn't something anybody could explain to you. It was something you caught on to when it came into your presence. Either you'd catch a piece of it and apply it to yourself or you'd let it pass you by and not even know that you missed it. Pepper Dash of Salt was confident. *He might not even know that he likes true women yet,* she thought to herself. She ate the tomato and cucumbers from the top of her salad as she waited. Dipped two croutons in the modest amount of ranch dressing on her tray. She wanted to look like she'd just gotten there when he arrived. And this was her seventh day in a row of Soup Factory lettuce, minestrone, and strawberry Jell-O, so he should better hurry up.

Chapter Twenty-Four

"Y'all better walk back quick so you make it home before it gets dark." He pulled an orange Zig-Zag pack from his pocket to check his supply. "I'm dry after this one, man." He looked at Richard.

"I have enough for us to float all night."

"Live, man," Tonio extended his hand and they bumped fists.

Tina crossed her arms over her chest and popped her hip.

"You making us walk home by ourselves, Anthony? That's a long ways."

"You walked an hour and a half here without me holding your hand, y'all can't make it home?" Tonio scratched his head with the plastic teeth of his pick.

"Y'all think you're grown anyway, grown your ass home," he added. Richard, Lavender, and the Bowen twins snickered.

"Y'all ready?" Tina turned her back to Tonio and looked at her girls. Everyone nodded.

"We better walk fast," Tasha-Marie said, then bent down to adjust the laces on her Keds.

The four girls started moving and Tina turned back.

"I'm telling Momma about this, Anthony, think I ain't."

"Shut your silly mouth up, Tina. Momma ain't gonna do nothing." He grinned. "Say something and see what happens."

"Check it out, man, your little sister's trying to punk you, man," Richard said, allowing his vato accent to flavor his words. "*Charleston Blue,* went to her head, man."

Tonio and Richard turned away from the girls and bumped fists again after walking a few lines in the concrete. Tonio turned around.

"Selah. You wanna come with us?" Tonio stood there in the middle of the sidewalk looking unrushed and calm, his black jeans just loose enough around his waist for Selah to see the thin blue line in his underwear waistband when he pulled up his white T-shirt to pat his stomach.

Selah looked at Tina with asking in her eyes.

"I wouldn't go if I was you," Tina said at a normal pitch. "That *asshole* might leave you somewhere."

"Now I'm the one that's telling Momma. She gonna wash out your mouth," Tonio teased, in a sing-songy voice. "What you gonna do, man?" He looked at Selah.

Tasha-Marie touched Selah's arm. "You should listen to Tina; she knows her brother better than you do. It might not be cool."

"I'll see you guys tonight when we get back to your house, all right, Tina?"

"See you at the house then, but I still wouldn't go," Tina said, shaking her head.

The Bowen brothers lived on the West Side of town; they made a right down Fifth Street as Tonio, Richard, Lavender, and Selah headed east toward Fifth Street Park. The four of them walked, Richard and Lavender in the front, Tonio and Selah in the back.

They didn't talk much, just strolled slowly, taking in the warm evening. Selah was excited though she tried not to show it. She reminded herself to walk with her back straight so not to show her stomach rolls and look twice as big as Lavender. Any time Tonio asked Selah something, she knew better than to say anything back to him. She just nodded yes or no and smirked her lips in a way that made it difficult to figure out whether she was experiencing pleasure or pain. Mama Gene always told Selah that it was better to look stupid than to open your mouth and prove it. So Selah kept her mouth closed like the rest of them did.

Selah had enough to think about that she didn't want to talk about anyway. By the time they got to the park, Selah realized it was only a couple of blocks from where Ruthie Mae lived—or used to live. Selah wasn't sure and Mama Gene rarely mentioned Selah's mom anymore. When she did, she said Ruthie Mae's name like she was talking about stomach cancer. Selah wondered what her mother would have thought seeing her hang out with the high schoolers. Selah thought that Ruthie would be proud of her for choosing a guy like Tonio. Tonio was fine, but he also had a strong street sense.

"Y'all want to kick it in the fortress?"

Tonio pointed across the park to a platform with a slide and three short metal walls.

"Why don't you and Selah go up there and me and Tammie will hang out by the lake."

"See you in a minute, bro," Tonio held up the peace sign on his right hand.

Though Selah was clearly with Tonio and Lavender was with Richard, it didn't feel like a date. Tonio and Selah walked with a good two feet of air between them and they rarely looked at each other. Tonio climbed up first and let Selah climb up behind him. Tonio chose his corner of the fortress and Selah sat diagonally across from him. It felt good to rest her feet again, but the three mounds protruding from the fortress floor made it difficult to find a good position.

Tonio took the orange zigzag folder out of his pocket. He looked in Selah's eyes for the first time.

"You smoke?"

Selah shook her head.

"Not really," she added as an afterthought.

"Not really or not ever?"

She shook her head again.

"I've smoked a cigarette before but never weed."

"A virgin; I love it."

Tonio laughed a crooked laugh. The kind of laugh she would expect him to have after he had already taken a few puffs.

Selah moved her legs from Indian style and braced her arms around her knees.

"You gonna try some with me?" Tonio asked.

She shrugged her shoulders and a nervous giggle slipped out of her mouth.

"You gonna try just a little bit for me?"

"A little maybe, I guess," she answered.

Tonio laid the thin white parchment-looking rectangle on the gray metal and took a clear baggie with a lot of seeds and a few shriveled green tuffs out of his back pocket. Tonio diligently picked away the seeds and spread the shriveled ware onto the sheet. With both hands he brought the white sheet up to his mouth and slid the tip of his tongue over one edge. With his thumb and his index finger he rolled the sheet until none of the green was showing and sealed it with his spit.

"When I was little," Tonio laughed to himself, "my daddy used to always tell me that dusk was the best time of the day to get a smoke on . . . I guess he was right because I am about to enjoy this like a mutha-fucka."

Selah gently knocked her head against the metal wall. She was surprised at herself for being envious of Tonio. *At least his father had told him something.*

"You wanna hit first?"

Selah shook her head no quickly. "You go first."

"You want me to teach you?" Tonio asked, his words dirty with seduction.

"Yeah," Selah said. That's what he wanted to hear.

Tonio grinned.

"Come sit by me then."

Selah scooted over to him on her butt and Tonio put his left arm around her shoulder. This was the first time he had touched her. Selah liked the feel of his arm on her body. Tonio put the joint in a clip and lit it.

"You wanna try it with the clip or without?"

"What's the difference?" Selah asked.

"Nothing really, I use the clip when the joint is a roach and might burn my fingers. I kinda like the way it looks though."

Selah nodded and watched Tonio take the clip to his mouth. He sucked. Then sucked again. Then held the air in his lungs for a long moment. "What you want to do," his words sounded gruff and disconnected, "what you want to do is get the shit deep into your lungs so that it penetrates."

"I'm not ready for deep."

"Just watch." Tonio took two more puffs for himself, then sucked hard and blew the smoke into Selah's mouth.

"Swallow," he said, "that'll get you high quick."

Selah swallowed inadvertently. She was caught up in the fact that Anthony Rayvon Perkins's lips had touched hers.

Tonio kept smoking until a pinch of the burned white paper was left. He put the clip to the side and in the next moment pressed his lips to hers like he knew her. Selah had wanted this, but she was startled by his lack of softness. As Tonio plunged his tongue into her mouth in hard, slobbery motions, Selah knew what Carla was talking about. Tonio's breath did stink, but it didn't smell like na-na, it smelled like burnt dry weeds, almost like Selah's hair smelled if Mama Gene pressed it too hard.

Tonio placed his whole right hand between Selah's thighs and groped her crotch like a batch of free candy. Selah squirmed.

"You like it like that, huh?"

She shrugged, wanting to push his hand away and not wanting to at the same time.

"Yeah, you like it hard, don't you?"

Selah knew that it didn't matter if she liked it. He liked it.

When Tonio moved from her mouth, Selah wiped the wetness from her face.

"Take these tight ass pants off."

He was talking to himself.

Tonio busted the top button of her favorite pants and the other four buttons slipped out of their slits quickly. This was supposed to be romantic, her first time. It was supposed to be with Tonio, but not this Tonio. It was supposed to be with the Tonio who ate an orange without his fingers rupturing its tender flesh. It was supposed to be with the laid-back Tonio who did his math homework in English class and would rather go to detention than run for a class if he was late. That Tonio, the one who was supposed to savor Selah like his morning milk and cookies and make her his girlfriend some day.

Selah's Bed

Tonio pulled one of Selah's legs from her pants and let the blue pants dangle attached to her ankle. He shoved three fingers in her dry pussy, after four deep pumps, he pushed in his dick. This was not girlfriend sex, it was something else. Selah held her fist balled tight and tried not to give in to the impulse to cry. Didn't he know that thirteen-year-old vaginas weren't ripe yet?

When he was done, Tonio brushed her sweaty bangs from her face with his hand and disengaged himself. He fell off of her and rested his head against the cooling metal before zipping his pants.

Selah lay there on the hard mounds. With her eyes closed and her breath only existing on the inside. She felt a faint rumble beneath her.

"You save some for me?" Richard said with energy, popping through the hole into the fortress.

"Ask her," Tonio said, still resting his head.

Richard squatted down and balanced his weight on the balls of his feet; his black jeans covered the front of his shoes. He glanced over - Selah's partially clothed, unmoving body.

"I'll pay you a quarter, little girl, if you give me some." He looked at her then back at Tonio. "Was she good?"

Tonio shrugged his shoulders.

"Was she good as her momma?"

"Richard, man. That's wrong, man, that's wrong. She probably - don't even know about that, man."

Selah didn't move until they told her to, and even then it took her time to climb back into her body, replace her clothes, and disappear again.

Chapter Twenty-Five

"Give me my medicine, Mathis," she said, in not quite a whisper.

Mama Gene leaned into the darkness on her extended left arm, zeroing in on Papa Frank's sleeping silhouette.

"Shhh."

Papa Frank adjusted his pillow so that the slobber that had collected on his yellow pillowcase when he slept wasn't touching his face.

"Mathis, don't have me shoot your half-witted behind in your sleep. I know where you keep that .22. I asked you for my medicine. Why did you take all of my bottles?"

"Woman, I'm sleep."

Papa Frank rolled over and lined his body on the opposite edge of the full-size bed. He pulled the blue sheet and scrap material quilt tight over his ears.

Whenever Selah walked in the room and saw Mama Gene and Papa Frank sleeping, she thought that Mama Gene looked like a thick piece of salt pork and Papa Frank looked like a thin piece of cooked bacon under the covers.

Mama Gene flipped on the light, then propped her pillow in a beige case between her back and the headboard. She pulled her Sunday crossword puzzle from the nightstand drawer and sat it on her lap without a pencil.

"Woman it's two o'clock in the morning and I'll be damned if - you're gonna wake up the whole house just because you're coming down off your fix."

"Mathis my doctor gave me those pills. A licensed physician. You know what happened to my back and you're not a doctor so you should leave my medicine alone."

"Pills," Papa Frank said edging the cover up over his eyes.

She snatched the quilt off of his body and Papa Frank threw the sheet off himself when he popped up to a sitting position in one swoop.

"You ain't gonna do this shit tonight, Eugenia. You take your irritated, no pill having behind to sleep. I only have one more good hour of rest before I gotta get to work."

Mama Gene smoothed the wrinkled newspaper with her palm.

"Well, as far as I am concerned, I think you've slept all you're going to sleep for the night."

"Well, I think you've taken just about all the pills you're gonna take for the evening as well, so we're even."

He lay back on his back and put his hands over the fly of his striped linen pajama bottoms. Mama Gene sat there silent for a moment. She spoke almost softly when she spoke.

"Just give me two of the fours, Frank, and I'll go on back to sleep."

"I don't have your pills, Eugenia. Ain't no use in you asking."

"Please, Frank. Spasms are shooting up my back. Just two white ones, Frank."

Papa Frank knew that she was only supposed to take one white pill every four to six hours and he had seen her take three at one time and one heart-shaped pink pill as he was getting ready for bed at eight thirty. Maybe it was time for her to take them again, but she'd have to go out to his truck to get them.

Papa Frank shrugged his shoulders and pulled the disheveled covers back onto his body.

"I don't know what to tell you, Eugenia; I guess you're gonna have to drink some orange juice or eat some of these lima beans you cooked to calm you down."

It was no use. She wasn't going to win with Papa Frank and she knew it. Let his frail looking, burnt piece of bacon, bony-shouldered-ass sleep then. And if he could sleep through all the noise she was about to make taking all the pots out of the refrigerator and throwing away those lima beans and neck bones he intended to take to work in the morning, more power to him.

Chapter Twenty-Six

Selah knew how to work red lights and black magic. She walked upstairs and closed the darkroom door behind her. She was excited about these pictures. She wanted to see if the camera tasted the same knot she did when she saw him.

She knew she would run into him last week, she felt it in her bones. And Pepper Dash of Salt said yes, but she'd have to wait four full days. Selah spent those days unrushed like chewing tobacco. She needed to think this through. She'd never been attracted to one of her clients the way she was attracted to him. Usually when she photographed someone the energy was clean, but she had muddied her power with her cross intentions.

Selah had managed to keep business and sexual attraction separate because something in her conscience would short-circuit her desire well before she entered the studio with camera in hand. The man, any man, would become a specimen; the vehicle she saw life through for that moment and nothing else. And despite all of this, she was developing a knot for him.

She realized that she had developed a knot for one man before now. The knot was her green light. A special man could turn the stresses of her life into liquid fire. This is where Selah messed up because Parker was the only man she had ever shot nude and felt this kind of thing for. And he had only let her do it once, while they were both still in college. That was the day she fell in love. Selah should have known. She should have made Pepper Dash of Salt her lover and left the camera out of it.

The camera had a different kind of power. The camera could cast a spell and make the temporary look permanent, ugly, beautiful. She was about to get-got and she dressed for it that day taking the time not to put on underwear.

Chapter Twenty-Seven

She trailed behind Tonio and Richard. By the time they reached the edge of the Kmart parking lot, with three solid blocks left to walk, Selah understood at thirteen what most people never grasp their entire lives—crazy isn't a difficult place to get to.

Some people snap off into crazy like a carrot, making a clean, crisp break. Others save into it like a pension or blue-chip stamps, building up their investment until they eventually earn the right to its benefits. Selah didn't know at this point how she got here; she - didn't know that there would be other events in her life that would cause her to return here, but she knew where she was. She was in the place on the inside of herself where hurt people go. A safe place. A small place. A place with tiny air holes that lead out but don't let the pain of the outside back in.

It would be weeks before she left this place. Weeks before Mama Gene's touch connected with the world that coursed underneath her skin. Her teachers would notice the shell of a girl left behind, so would Tasha-Marie, Tina, and Carla, but no one knew that a thirteen year old could die behind big brown eyes and smile through the gap in her teeth at the same time.

Selah walked home this way. Tucked behind blue bell-bottoms with dirt tracks traveling up her legs and across her backside. She - didn't notice the missing button anymore or how the delicate elastic band of her white flowered underwear showed above her waistband. She didn't feel the soft trickles of blood seep through the cotton crotch into the blue polyester, making an avant-garde stain with moist red edges that would turn stale and brown. All Selah could hear was the silence, like what happens when an airplane changes altitude too quickly. This bloated feeling inside of her was a blessing. The only thought that occurred to her as she followed the frames of Tonio and Richard as they turned rolled grass into white smoke in the evening air, is that this is what God must feel like when he is angry.

Chapter Twenty-Eight

At first it wasn't even Alzheimer's that Selah was afraid of; it was the pills, the cosmetic concoctions that Mama Gene assembled in the private loneliness of her own home. Selah found it hard to fault Mama Gene; she had fallen to the occasional feel-better-pill-pop-and-fix-all drink herself. But more than anything, Selah did with sex what Mama Gene had done with prescription meds most of her adult life. Selah understood the sadness and powerlessness of her grandmother's situation. She understood telling herself enough was enough and she'd never do it again, then having to wipe the sex from between her legs. Selah had even prayed to God's turned back and asked him to please take away her desire for the only relief she knew. She knew what Mama Gene's prayers must have sounded like. She had to know. The prayers from rock bottom, even for the most non-believing addict, were some of the purest prayers there were, second only to the plea for life.

Mama Gene was past prayer when Selah moved her into her

house. Mama Gene would have sold stolen Gideon Bibles to get her fix. Selah didn't know how serious the situation was until Mama Gene ended up in Community Hospital overdosed with a bruised hip.

The room did not smell of blood and guts, or any of the other gory details associated with emergency rooms. It smelled sterile like tears, salt, and fear. The same smell Selah would notice almost a year later when she permanently enrolled Mama Gene into Sweet Home Convalescent Hospital. What scared Selah the most were the tubes running in and out of Mama Gene's body. Selah could have dealt with a broken arm or anything else she could see. If she could have seen Mama Gene's problem, she could have visualized its repair on the backside of her eyes. But even with the bruised hip, what was going on with Mama Gene was happening on the inside.

A clear slinky tube connected Mama Gene's mouth to a computerized respirator. There were tubes in her nose. Tubes running two different types of fluid into her right arm from plastic baggies attached to something that looked like a five-pronged metal coat rack. Selah took in Mama Gene's eyes. They looked deep. Still. Like murky water shaded by leaves so that the sun could not get through. There was no swimming in them. Her face was inflated twice its normal size and her eyes hung back in their sockets like rotting sea kelp, knotted and twisted, sinking farther down instead of rising back up. When Selah stared in close, nothing registered. Mama Gene wasn't there. She had left. Like Selah used to do as a young girl when she disappeared into crazy, leaving only the gapped-tooth smile she'd inherited from Mama Gene to prove that she'd been there. And Selah could have been okay with this, but Mama Gene had never disappeared like this before, and Selah didn't know if she knew how to get back.

Selah's Bed

"I'm here, Mama Gene."

Selah paused and stared a beam of concentration into Mama - Gene's eyes.

"Don't you go and die on me, Momma. I need you. You're the only person, only one . . ."

Selah tried to breathe past thickness developing in her nose. A nurse kindly came by and placed clear tape on Mama Gene's eyelids so that Selah couldn't feel the haunt of death standing at attention behind them.

She was cold to the touch. A mass of barely formed brownness on a stretcher, under a single blanket, with coal black lines drawn on both of her shoulders.

The questions weren't immediate. They came minutes later when someone figured Selah had had enough time to grieve. "Did you know your grandmother was suicidal? Was this her first attempt? Which drugs does she take? Does she combine them often? Can you retrieve all of her bottles so that we can figure out everything she took? Are you going to have power of attorney?

Suicidal? Power of attorney? Selah couldn't hear any of them. She just walked away, back to her grandmother's taped eyelids. Selah - didn't need to answer questions right now. She had questions. And the only person who could answer them was Mama Gene.

Selah stayed in the emergency room for three more hours before the hospital staff was able to move Mama Gene to intensive care. Selah knew they didn't expect her to live. The way she saw it, they - didn't expect most of the patients who entered intensive care to live. The message was written all over—in the tired faces of the staff, the darkness of the eight-patient unit with beds arranged in a half moon, the self-activated morphine drips hanging from bedsides, the tubes. But mostly the message was in the quiet, clean pamphlets that hung crisp and folded in plastic holders in hallways and waiting rooms about how to deal with the death of a loved one.

"Parker, I won't be home tonight. I don't know when I'll be home. Mama Gene is in the hospital from a drug overdose. I'll call you when I can. I'm at Community Hospital." Selah thought *I love you,* but she didn't say it; there was too much going on in her head to figure out her reason.

Chapter Twenty-Nine

Selah had prepared the stop bath and fixer; now it was time to mix the developer. She placed the graduate of developer into cool water for it to stabilize at 68 degrees, then poured it into the tray. She was still nude when she did this. She was usually clothed and composed during this part. She normally developed pictures at her home studio and not at the office on Degnan Boulevard, but not today. She needed to see what had just happened to her and the roll of film on the counter was the only way to do it.

The trays were arranged in front of her from left to right: developer, stop bath, fixer. Selah tied a pink scarf around her sweaty, puffed up hair then washed her hands without putting on moisturizer. Her hands had to be dry for this. After turning off the white lights, she opened the package of paper in a wash of red. She prepared the negative, then with her left hand she slid the paper into the developer and rocked the tray for one minute.

Selah wasn't happy or sad right now. She put the wet sheet into the stop bath, then fixer, and turned the lights back on while the sheet was still in the tray. After washing and sponging down the sheet, she walked back into the dim sexed air of the studio and sat under her photograph of the crying drummer with the proof between her legs on the carpet. A bead of latent sweat rolled between her breasts.

He was beautiful. She hadn't imagined it. Selah had made love to a few men in her day, but he was not just making love to her. He had pried her open with his spit then shined her until she ached from the inside out. And though Selah wanted to make herself feel special, though she wanted to believe that she had whipped some mojo on him that had caused him to lose his damned mind, she knew he would have done the same for any woman.

Another lover *thought* he had done that to her. Spit-shined her uterus so that she would always come back to him and his pit bull that he never made leave the room during sex. He thought he had worked her so good that his saliva had edited her DNA and any time she thought of home she would think of his dick inside her as home. - That's why she believed he called his penis *Homebase*. But he needed her and she knew it. Needed her like a husband needed a wife and she already had a husband.

She laughed at herself and tried to pull up a strand of the tightly woven industrial carpet. Selah held the proof close to her face. Pepper Dash of Salt reminded her of Parker if she looked at him from a certain angle. He was thin and his skin was smooth like Parker's. His waist muscles were compact, yet long like Parker's. And he could open her vaginal lips and blow in sunshine by touching her with one finger like Parker used to be able to do when he had cared enough to harness his magic.

But this was not Parker; this was Peter. Peter Couday, a black man from Louisiana who said his name with angels on his shoulder and a pitch fork on his breath. Peter Couday, who would travel Selah Wells like an overused AAA map until she knew where her home was.

Selah's whole body was sore, like three days after her first day back at the gym. She set the proof and magnifying glass aside and let her head fall back until it touched the wall. Peter Couday, she said low and deep. She slid her full hand between her thighs and pressed her index finger hard to her clitoris. A jolt ran through her body. Peter Couday, she said again, moving her hand in a circular motion between her legs. Selah's vaginal lips were still engorged from the way he had repetitiously pulled his penis out of her until it almost disengaged, then slid it back in slowly like he was playing smoky jazz on a trombone.

Her hair left a round stain on the wall. She lay on her back and bent her legs at the knees in the air. She wanted to relive it. He had mounted her, her hip pinned against the base of the wall, her wrists held tight under one of his hands as he held her butt cheeks with the other and maneuvered himself into her. Selah crossed her legs at the ankles and bucked the same way she had when Peter was inside her. She bucked again, squeezing her buttocks tight. She remembered the way he had bit her neck to force her into submission. She had pretended to submit. When he let go of her neck, she snatched her right hand free and socked him hard in the chest.

"Fuck me, mutha fucka," she had said, almost hyperventilating from the thick air between them.

He grabbed her hand again and started to move his pelvis in a slow grind.

"I can take it," she said, staring him defiantly in the eye.

"You only think you can." He licked the sweat from her cheek with his flat tongue, then sucked her bottom lip into his mouth.

She tried to get away. She tried to pull her wrists from his grasp and break free.

"You're going to bust open your knee if you keep hitting that wall like that," he said, continuing the paced rotation of his hips. "Just let me have you. Or fight me. I like it both ways."

Chapter Thirty

Selah didn't have the courage to go home. It was something about how she looked and smelled of dried-up sex that made her know she couldn't. *Mama Gene will smell the blood,* she thought. Selah had never hoped for grand things in her life. She didn't know that borrowing eggs and dollar rides were a form of female survival. But Selah had left the mundane by default. She was now a savoir. The little girl turned woman who would rescue her grandmother from fearing the things her granddaughter would one day become.

As her body dented to the metal mounds and grains of sand scratched her back, Selah didn't look into Tonio's eyes. But when she looked into Richard's, underneath the haze of reefer and pheromones, she saw what he thought of her. Even as an adult, looking back on the entirety of her decisions, Selah had never considered herself a whore. She figured the odds would have been better if she had been. Selah imagined that a whore still felt something when she washed bodily fluids from her pubic hair. That a whore got tired of her body being pounded by the strangeness of hardened regret. But Selah only had one regret. One regret that turned her into a woman that felt most alive under the weight of man-handling hands that rendered something like pleasure.

Tonio held the white, wood-framed screen door open with his back as he fished for the single front door key in his front pocket. He hadn't said a word to Selah since moments after he had pried her open like a jammed bottom locker at the skating rink. How many times had Selah put in a quarter and not been able to turn and pull the round, orange-tipped key from its slot. How many times had she kicked the protruding orange cap with the side of the metal skate wheels and hoped to break the locker in if she couldn't get her money's worth. But Tonio didn't have to break Selah in and he knew that. He knew because of the way she smiled five centimeters too big, open and gap toothed, hiding her sweaty hands behind her back whenever he sat across from her on the loveseat. He knew because she gave up pork rinds and stopped eating pickled pig's feet from the jar in his presence because he said it gave her glutton breath. Even if - he'd never read the inside of her yellow pee chee folders, he knew. And he broke her anyway, because he could.

Tonio grabbed a bag of Oreo cookies from the kitchen cabinet and left Selah standing at the door as he navigated his way through the darkness to his room on Frieda Perkins's side of the house. Richard - didn't mind to muffle his *shit-fuck* combination when his kneecap hit the corner of the coffee table on his way to the couch. He would crash there tonight. His sleeping body would slump into the flattened middle cushion the same way Selah's behind did when she sat next to Tina watching episodes of *Sanford and Son* on Friday nights.

Walking up the stairs, Selah became aware of the pain between her legs. She turned right, instead of left toward Tina and Anne's room.

She held the bathroom doorknob with both hands and pushed it gently until it clicked closed. She didn't want to turn on the lights. She - didn't want to see the saliva lines of Tonio's sloppy kisses crisscross the area around her lips. Selah unfastened the blue bell-bottoms and pulled them down slowly over the ache in her hips. When she tried to pull down her underwear, blood had partially dried and attached itself to the coarse yet tender vaginal hair between her thighs. Selah pulled the panties' crotch away from her skin like she would have a Band-Aid from her forearm, cautiously, feeling the hairs pull white in their sockets then back into place.

She sat in the dark on the toilet, her legs pressed tightly together, her left hand clutching the metal arm of the empty toilet tissue holder. Selah bit both sides of her cheeks so not to scream. The warm liquid came out in spurts that burned with each salty pass through her vaginal lips. Her fingers fumbled about the counter for tissue and found the empty cardboard center. Selah pulled a face cloth from the towel bar on the wall behind her. The towel was damp and still smelled of Ivory soap. She wiped it across her face then between her legs. Her vagina was a pussed-over bruise. Selah clenched her teeth as the towel stung her skin. She would take a bath. She would sit naked in the dirt-ringed tub and let water fill to the rim. She would dunk her freshly pressed hair under with the rest of her body and hold her breath until the water had had its way with the remainder of Tonio's touch.

Chapter Thirty-One

A hospital chair was the most comfortable place between life and death for Selah to live in. She stayed there for three days in the same sour underwear and broken-in denim. Selah purchased a stick of deodorant and toothbrush from the gift shop. She washed her face in the lobby bathroom as did the members of the Samoan family camping out in the waiting room to be near Marta Tusitala in bed six.

Selah acknowledged for the smallest moment that maybe God - hadn't forgotten her completely. Selah sat in the waiting room among the sleeping bags and pillows shoved into corners. Chairs had been moved away from walls and arranged so that the cushions formed a land bridge connecting between the butt and the legs. This was not a welcoming place. The rooms were never warm and nothing seemed anything like home. Some people had spent most of their lives in and out of these walls, Selah thought. Their skin had thickened to the coldness and their butts had grown more padding and tolerance for the discomfort. She felt like a camel. She drank little other than water and chewed on licorice to keep sugar in her system. Selah figured she could go through weeks of this if she had to. She would cancel her meetings and shoots in order to be with her grandmother. Mama Gene had been the only person in her life whom she could trust enough to need.

So Selah called on God—Jesus, Jah, Jehovah, Yahweh, Allah, Buddha, Ancestors. She breathed, chanted, raised hands, laid hands, marked her forehead with virgin olive oil. She would have burned sage over her shoulder if she'd had some. Only thing she couldn't do was cry.

Selah had almost fallen asleep in the chair next to Mama Gene's bed when she saw the slightest movement in Mama Gene's finger.

"Mama Gene," Selah said, grabbing her hand quickly and gently. "Do it again for me, Mama Gene; move your finger."

Selah laid Mama Gene's hand flat onto hers and waited. After several moments her finger moved.

"Thank you Jesus," Selah said, then bent to kiss the tape over Mama Gene's cheek.

Later that evening, Mama Gene would move her feet. Two days later, she would open her eyes, but she still wouldn't be able to see. And though the tubes were still in her mouth and she couldn't speak, Selah would buy her grandmother a note pad, and within one week, Mama Gene would be writing again at a second grade level.

Chapter Thirty-Two

Peter liked to suck Selah's toes. Suck, suck, not lick, lick. He wasn't afraid of dirty heels and toe jam. He embraced his task fully, never skimping or moving over any ridge or rough patch too quickly.

"You have serious issues . . ." Selah said, then paused to absorb the feeling of all five of her toes and half of her arch in his mouth. ". . . but you know what you're doing." Selah let her shoulders collapse back to the blanketed floor. "This should be a service offered at the end of a pedicure," she added as an afterthought.

Peter did know what he was doing. He'd been sucking toes since he was sixteen and fell in deep like with a volleyball player with a weak ankle and sore feet. The temptation of musk, shape, and beauty was too much for Peter to resist.

Peter barely looked at Selah's face when he did this.

"If I didn't have pretty feet, I would sho' nuf think something was really wrong with you."

Peter never responded to Selah's chiding; he took it as his applause and encouragement. He stood up. His six foot tall, nude body towered over her. Peter held out his hand.

"Give me your foot."

Selah flipped her moist foot into the air. Leg fully extended, her toes hit his crotch area. He placed her foot in his hand and commenced to grind his balls on her heel. The movement of his hips got Selah aroused. Dip then circle. Dip then circle. Peter bent at the waist. He flicked her toes forward with his tongue then commenced to suck the back meat of each toe.

"Get the hell off my foot," Selah said, acting mad because he was pushing her over the edge.

"Relax and pay attention," he said, meeting her attitude.

Peter took one kneecap to the back of her knee and started to grind the sensitive skin behind her patella.

"Don't have me hurt you, Peter."

"Let me hurt you," he said back.

Selah gave up. *Let go and let God,* she thought to herself.

She had almost drifted into a heavy Tuesday morning sleep when Peter poured two drops of chilled water from the water cooler between her breasts.

"Stop playing."

"I thought you were thirsty."

Selah took the water and sat up. She dipped her fingers in the cup and splashed his face before she drank.

"My husband did that to me once when we were younger. Just once and he never tried it again."

Peter gulped down an entire cup of water.

"Don't tell me, you threatened divorce."

"No, we weren't even married yet," Selah half smiled. "Those days were like eating the last battered pork chop and knowing that there's one left in the pot."

Peter scooped Selah in his arms and held her waist.

"You know what they say, you can't cry over powdered sugar falling off of a stale donut."

That was a lie—Selah knew that you could. She'd been doing it most of her life.

"I guess not everybody's like you," she said solemnly.

Peter kissed the side of her face.

"You gotta learn to let things go. I've left a lot of things behind in my life. I ain't proud of it, but I can't live my life backward neither. Life is short and death is certain."

"You've never lost a child." She shook her head. "You couldn't say that if you had. It's the worst thing in the world."

Peter hugged her tighter. "I'm sorry to hear that. Boy or girl?"

"Girl. A little girl."

"How old was she when it happened?"

Selah turned her neck to look Peter in the eye.

"She was too young. I was young. I just didn't think that my life would end up like this. I never intended to cheat on my husband. I wanted more kids and—"

"You don't need to explain yourself to me."

"I want you to know who you're with," she said still staring him in the eye. "I'm not dependable in the ways that a normal woman should be. I'm like a passing-through woman. Only thing I'm faithful to is my pain."

"Shhhh," he said, and kissed her right cheek. She was speaking to a passing-through man.

Chapter Thirty-Three

March 17, 1978

When you are three days old, your fingers will be tiny and wrinkled. Mama Gene showed me pictures once of my momma when she was a baby and she was the same way. Prune-like with no hair, just a little soft fuzz around the hairline. Your hands will be the size of half my index finger and you will keep them balled into tight fists because you listened to what I told you.

You are better than the blackberry lemonade Grandma used to make for the two of us. The secret was to squish the berries between your fingers, add more lime than lemon and a small drop of blackstrap molasses. You are sweeter than all of that.

I have already bought Vaseline to rub on your skin to stop the chaffing. Mama Gene says that all babies look ashy with splotches when they come out of the womb. I bought the Vaseline anyway, but I don't believe her. You glisten with the sheen of a Sugar Daddy toffee stick after it has been licked four good times.

Jenoyne Adams

I cry because I realize you are mine. I will give birth to you out of my body. Your name will be Sasha. Mama Gene said Sasha ain't a black name. I wrote Michelle Sasha Lareaux on a piece of lined paper and taped it to my dresser mirror. Maybe you don't need a black name. Maybe I should name you the furthest thing from black like Anastasia or Penelope. I'm thinking you might be a dancer, something tall and regal when you grow up. But secretly I hope you will stay my little girl. Stay dependent on me first. I'm looking forward to placing bows and barrettes in your hair, ribbons. Talking baby talk with you, teaching you how to say Momma.

You know who I am. I think you already know my voice. I am promising you today that I will be a good mommy. I will love you and take you to the park. Sing to you at night, walk you to school. Lay your clothes out every morning and listen to you when you want to wear the same shirt over and over for days at a time. I will wash that shirt every night if I have to. You will know you are important to me. Something I know my mother would have shown me had she been around. And even though Mama Gene says that she already raised her child and her grandchild, and that she's not going to raise a great-grand, she won't have to raise you. You'll have me to do everything for you and she can help out sometimes when she feels like it. She says I am naïve. That this is the hardest job I will ever do and that sleeping on rocks isn't the same as eating them. I pretended not to be listening.

Chapter Thirty-Four

It was Mrs. Perkins who had found Mama Gene passed out on the floor of her bedroom. As much as Mama Gene loved Mrs. Perkins's daughter Anne, Mama Gene couldn't stand Mrs. Perkins. She'd been hating that woman since way back in the day when Mama Gene first saw her plastic-covered couches. So when Selah found out that Frieda Perkins had a spare set of keys to Mama Gene's house, she knew something was wrong. Mama Gene hadn't been getting around well for about a year at this point. She was seventy-five and her memory wasn't so great. She found it hard to stand and walk for long periods of time. Even a trip to the grocery store two blocks down the street had gotten to be too much for her.

Mama Gene's life had gotten pretty simple. Meals-on-Wheels delivered one meal per day and she lived within the confines of her social security check. Selah would help Mama Gene out here and there, mainly by driving out to buy her groceries every two weeks. Selah felt like she was misusing her grandmother sometimes. Like she was one of those ungrateful granddaughters who took and took growing up, but never gave back. In her heart she knew this wasn't true. Selah hated it when she had to tell Mama Gene that she didn't have any extra money to lend to her each month. Selah and Parker lived comfortably and what they couldn't buy in cash, they could buy with credit. But Selah had learned the hard way years ago—give Mama Gene money, she'll buy pills; give her merchandise—it disappears.

After the hospital stay, Selah knew it would be impossible for Mama Gene to go back to living alone. The mistakes had started to wear on Selah. How many times had Mama Gene placed paper plates in the hot oven or been in a drug-induced delirium when Selah called? How many times had she caught the bus and ended up sitting in front of the bank where her account had been closed five years before? The bank had gotten used to the routine, so when Mama Gene arrived, someone would page Selah the moment she walked through the doors. There'd been too many times and too many scares. Every time Selah drove to 522 Sycamore, she got an ache in her memory. This was not the same Mama Gene who had raised her.

Selah would keep her word to her grandmother. She promised to never make her live in a nursing home. Mama Gene had worked in damn near every convalescent hospital in San Bernardino, and she knew things Selah didn't.

"Don't you ever make me go there, Selah. Never make me go to a home, Selah," Mama Gene said from her hospital bed three weeks after her overdose, which Selah would soon find out was her second overdose on record at Community Hospital. Mama Gene's voice was weak. The doctor and respiratory specialist had only hours before taken the balloon from her throat and her vocal cords were still sore.

"I raised you bet-ter than that. We don't sac-ri-fice our old peo-ple like those white peo-ple do. We take care of them."

"Shhh. Rest yourself, Mama Gene; you've—just rest yourself."

"No," she forced out, her anger coming with it. "You promise me or they can just kill me right here. I won't live in no home. I won't."

Selah promised her grandmother, knowing that there was nothing else she could have said in that moment. When Mama Gene moved into the house with her, Selah learned new intimacies with her grandmother. She bathed her grandmother during recovery. She sponged dirt from under her deflated brown breasts. Changed her Depends. Dressed her every morning and placed her in her pajamas at night. All the time knowing, no matter how much brown sugar and love she poured into Mama Gene's oatmeal, that she had lied. Selah feared Mama Gene because now she knew her grandmother's potential—Mama Gene could remove herself permanently from Selah's life at any time. Without asking.

Chapter Thirty-Five

"You let him do you, didn't you?" Tina said, her morning breath hitting Selah's eyeballs. They lay on Tina's bed facing each other, a ruffle of blanket blocking Selah's mouth from Tina's stare.

Selah nodded, looking Tina intently in the eyes. There was no judgment. Selah was happy about that, but even though Tonio was her brother, Selah had expected Tina to be excited for her. Selah was the first of her crew to go all the way. Tina wasn't excited; she was calm.

Tina raised her head over Selah's body to make sure that Anne was still asleep.

"Was it all right?" she said, scooting her head closer to Selah's and lowering her voice. "He was nice to you, wasn't he?"

Selah shrugged her shoulders and nodded her head yes again.

"That's good," Tina half-smiled. "Tonio isn't very nice and he can be rough when he wants to be, so that's good. Did you like it?"

Selah pretended to need a moment to think.

"Not really." She shook her head, her voice cracking through the soreness in her throat.

"Do you like being a woman now?"

Selah shook her head no again.

"I don't think I'd like it either."

Tina paused to think of her next question. Selah kept her eyes on Tina's as she thought. Selah had never realized how much Tonio and Tina looked alike. Eyes that were wider at the bottom than they were at the top so that they resembled gumdrops.

"Did you know why he took you there?"

Selah crushed the ruffle in the blanket under her hand.

"I just wanted to go, Tina. I liked Tonio. I thought he was . . . I just thought maybe it would have been different."

"Did he wear a condom?"

"I don't know."

"You should always make a guy wear a condom, like him or not. Did you like the way his dick looked?"

"I didn't really see it; I didn't even touch it."

"I've touched one before." Tina checked for Anne again. "It looks and feels like a thick brown worm with loose skin. Almost like an earthworm."

Tina breathed in slow through her nostrils, then giggled.

"You know your hair is gonna matt up if you don't condition it and comb it out good. I'll do it before you go home if you want so Mama Gene don't kill you."

Something was different about Tina. Like Selah becoming a woman had opened up a part of Tina that had been closed to her before. Tina was mature and concerned like an adult friend would be. Like someone who knew you had made a mistake but had enough restraint within herself not to throw your error in your face. Tina was way more woman than Selah was. And Selah wondered how long she had been this way.

When she finally cried, two weeks later, only then did she feel it. The strain of her head stuck between a metal mound and silver wall. Only then did she smell his breath again, sweet and funky with weed, and the after-taste of buttered popcorn on his tongue. As she sat on her bed, blacking out *Selah loves Tonio* from the inside of her folders, she wished that she hadn't traded in multiple ponytails and ribbons so early. She wished that Tonio had kept his G.I. Joe longer and that her Holly Hobbie oven still had magic. But more than anything, she wished that her best friend didn't have gumdrop eyes that reminded her of her brother.

Chapter Thirty-Six

Had Selah seriously thought about it, she would have gone to look for Ruthie Mae, to tell her that her mother was sick. She would have driven down Baseline, south on Mount Vernon, through Little Mexico, past Fifth Street, and over the viaduct. If Selah had done this on a Friday night, right around six, driven slowly past the old thrift store off of Congress Street, she would have seen her mother hustling her body to the front cab of a gray pickup.

"Ay mommie, how much you cost me."

Ruthie Mae knew that black flesh was more refreshing than bottomless beer after working at the railroad all day. Even sagging black flesh, that fit into tight stretch pants like ground sausage filling its skin.

Selah would have found out that her mother could be bought and passed like good tequila for less money than Selah had in her wallet that day. But she didn't go. Way in the back of herself she remembered what Richard had said that day. *Was she good as her momma?* Selah knew what Richard would never find out. Selah was better.

Chapter Thirty-Seven

"You ever walk in on somebody while they were praying for you?" Selah asked Peter while she looked through an accordion file filled with old photographs.

"I've heard a few folks bless my name—*That son of a motherless dog.*" Peter chuckled and his eyes tightened into tiny sparkles and the corners of his lips turned up and in.

"You know that's not what I meant." Selah smiled.

"Gurrrl," he said sweet and long, "come back over here and let me hug on your bones."

Selah loved the way Peter's Louisiana flavor came out. It made her feel warm and safe, like how Parker used to lock his arm around her neck when they slept.

"I'm looking for something; you're gonna have to wait," she said.

Peter reached his hand out for Selah's foot and she kicked.

"Answer my question."

Peter rolled over on his back and placed his arms under his head.

"What do you mean, like my momma praying for me or something?"

Selah started on the next section of photos. "No, I mean like a lover. You ever hear up close a lover praying like she can save your life if she prays hard enough?"

Peter shook his head. "I ain't never much been into those religious gals. I like me a big ole sinner-type woman." He reached for her foot again.

"Is that what you think I am?"

"Well baby, you are kinda thick. What, has your husband been praying for you?"

"Yeah," Selah said, taking a close-up photo of her stomach when she was pregnant out of the file. "It felt like the house was shaking."

Selah remembered back to when Parker found her in the studio with another man. The next day she overheard him and Pastor Jackson in Parker's study casting the lust demon out of her. She would have normally been embarrassed, but the intensity and sincerity of his prayer had made her feel proud.

"So, you got your other man on your mind?"

"Why would you ask me something like that?" Selah frowned.

"I'm just trying to see if I can get in my time before you fade back to him."

Peter's smile was the kind of thing you want to jump into. Selah would often go up to him in the middle of shooting and give him a fat kiss on the lips. Nothing ever seemed to get under his skin and it had been two months since he'd been meeting her every Tuesday from nine to twelve in the morning for photographic sex and sweet-sour grapes from the vine in his backyard. They had simple needs with each other. They didn't bury each other with the weight of mortgages and savings interest.

Selah arched her foot toward him and wiggled her toes. "Baby, you want some more of this big toe?"

Peter laughed and grabbed her foot.

Selah liked his laugh. Peter had big laughter, clap your hands laughter. Laughter that looked too big to come out of such a thin and seemingly refined man. But Selah would learn over the course of months that Peter Couday was just honest. Honest in the kind of way that would one day hurt her feelings long after he had left the room and their joint smell had faded back into the Tuesday morning it came from.

Chapter Thirty-Eight

Selah wondered if there were girls in the world who weren't driven toward loving the way that she was. It was the dirty part of her that wanted it. The part that frowned on the inside when she thought of how small hands excited her skin.

She had been curious before. She had rolled her eyes up into her head when boys felt her T-shirt–covered mounds. She used to roll her eyes back hard and pretend like it hadn't happened. Later, when she was alone, she'd relive the experience as she flipped cool quarters in her pocket. The situation with Tonio pushed her full out. Twenty-five cents for shirt-covered breasts. Fifty for flesh. Seventy-five for a pants-down look. One dollar to place in a full finger.

It was a business. Something to occupy summer boredom until she made new friends. The Perkins house was still the hang-out house in the neighborhood. Selah missed coaxing Tina out of her hotbox room and watching Tonio eat oranges and do homework. Spending time with them had become part of her routine and now the routine was broken. Selah would often look through the window above her bed and see Carla and Tasha-Marie cutting through the grass toward Tina's back door. Selah still liked all of them. By the beginning of ninth grade she would start to spend time with Carla and Tasha-Marie again. Tonio had wronged Selah in a way that might have been normal to her had she already been a woman. But Selah was playing dress up, and Tina still had the eyes of her brother.

"No splits. If both of you want to stick in a finger, you both owe me a dollar first. No fifty-cent half fingers and no watching."

Selah was strict with the boys in an older sister kind of way, and for the most part the boys listened to her because she had what they wanted. The ones under thirteen often came back for seconds and thirds as their allowances and coin thievery allowed. They liked the brief feeling of a finger in her twat. Sometimes they would moan inadvertently or squish their nostrils up toward their eyes, but they'd come back again and again anyway. Their loyalty almost made her smile. She was aware that she wasn't the only girl in her neighborhood providing this service. Jackie Renee and her sister Brandy did it out of their home after school because Ms. Bradshaw didn't get home from work until six in the evening. Selah didn't consider the girls real competition. Their customers were mainly their older - brother's friends and both of the girls were still essentially flat-chested, unlike Selah.

The trash can area behind the Head Start building in front of the Waterman Gardens playground was Selah's beat. The area always smelled like old bananas and trash, but it was private—bricked in with two metal gates laced with a thin green plastic filling in its squares.

"You wait here," Selah said, pointing to Janice's twelve-year-old brother Leroi. "And don't you ever again, as long as your butt is black, knock on my grandma's door and ask for me. She'll kill the both us."

Mama Gene would have killed the both of them. That's why Selah did her dirt on the opposite side of the playground out of Mama Gene and Papa Frank's view. Selah knew Papa Frank wouldn't say anything even if he did find out. Ruthie Mae with all her leg climbing and manipulation had made life a living hell for Papa Frank while she grew up. Now, even if Selah was getting a beating out of this world, Papa Frank would never interfere. Papa Frank was the closest person to Mama Gene, and if he didn't put his pennies into her child-rearing business, everyone else had better know to stay out of it.

Selah didn't do much with the money she made. She bought herself candy occasionally and treated herself to fries and a Jumbo Jack from the Jack in the Box on the corner of Baseline and Waterman. More than anything she liked to count it and change the dollars in for quarters at the liquor store. She'd pour the change from the wrinkled paper bag onto the middle of her comforter, run her hands over the coins until her fingers picked up their gray tint. She'd think of her mother. Maybe this is what her mother did every night when she got home. Maybe she brought the men home with her sometimes. Selah didn't know. But now that she was experienced, she wasn't afraid of Tonio. Like him or not, she would have held her legs open wide for him like she used to do her smile.

Chapter Thirty-Nine

Mama Gene wasn't trying to kill herself. Not really. It was the heaviness in the center of her bones that she was trying to get away from. Some journeys aren't about forever. Some you don't even pack for, you just go. She was aware of herself when she went there. This kind of being intrigued her, the transformation from someone to something weightless. She wasn't Eugenia Wells, widow of a man she never married in the first place. She wasn't the mother of a woman who was paid for in pieces. She didn't have to think about growing old alone or notice degrees of herself disappear in real time. The pills softened her fall into a cataclysmic float. The letting go was beautiful—flesh from bone, bone from spirit, spirit to air.

So no, she wasn't afraid of dying. She had lived all of her deaths; the waking moments reminded her of them. She fought being awake like young children fight sleep. Crossed lines are inevitable when you live this way. Mistakes are guilty gifts that those left behind calculate.

Selah's Bed

•　•　•

The day of the overdose she had slipped. Slipped away into otherness the same way she had the night Papa Frank died lying next to her under a yellow sheet. He didn't fight with her about the pills that day. He had lost the strength for fighting months before. Once he'd even searched the tool case behind the long seat of his truck for a bottle of muscle relaxants to shut her up. Papa Frank knew more than anybody that peace could cost more than it was supposed to and still be worth it. But she would have to pay her own costs, he had told himself. She would have to find her own line and stick to the right of it to save herself.

Papa Frank had striven to be a martyr and savior. With tandem authority he had hid pills, called doctors, cried. The day he called the pharmacies and found thirteen prescriptions in her name between San Bernardino and Colton, he knew the pills were more important to her than he was. He hadn't even tried Rialto yet. He would never try Rialto; too much information could change his heart in a way that would make touching her impossible. Papa Frank loved Mama Gene too much to let his affections turn. So he ignored the pill bottles hidden in strange places and covered up her catatonic states with pass-out drinking of his own. He stopped hoping for cures and strength. Mumbled prayers and tears, he figured out, were for believers. All he longed for now was one thing: God please take us both at the same time.

Mama Gene was left with Papa Frank's Stingy Brim and clothes hanging in the closet the same way they had for forty-some years. She never drank out of the mason jar he filled with Lipton tea and a ring of sugar that settled on the bottom. She didn't move the can of Barbisol from the medicine cabinet or the screw-top bottle left on his side of the couch wrapped in a brown paper sack. These things reminded her of his death. The worst one she would ever face because she had heard his prayers.

For as long as she could remember, his syncopated snore and rough-skinned feet had accompanied her to sleep at night. When Papa Frank got up at four A.M. for work, Mama Gene used to roll over to his side of the bed to feel his warmth still harbored in the sheets. She knew when she was supposed to go. And she waited sober and hopeful for two weeks. She washed all of her and Papa - Frank's dirty clothes from the bathroom hamper. She threw away the covered mustard greens and ham hocks left in the refrigerator, folded the used pieces of tinfoil into polite squares, and placed them in the drawer with the plastic wrap. All she asked was, "God take me now," and she smiled graciously in the asking.

When nothing happened, she knew it was her fault. Had she not taken so many pills that night she could have helped him. She could have seen what was happening for what it really was: He was dying. Instead, his grunted pleas became the melody she drifted on. His rolled-back eyes and fist jabbing her side were reminders to fly higher. Papa Frank convulsed, his head knocking the headboard off beat as she drifted in and out of his passing without ever noticing the rumination of death.

She rolled that night around her mouth for six months as she walked through the rooms of the apartment in her linen housecoat with pearlized snaps. He was not there. She did not catch a glimpse of him through the cracked bathroom door. She never sat in the living room and heard the familiar crack of ice separating in the old school metal ice tray with pull-back lever. His things were there. The earthworms in the white Styrofoam container with holes punched in the top could have still been alive, but he wasn't.

This is what she thought about as she sat on yellow sheets with her back against the headboard. Ten Diazepam and twelve Hydrocodone sat in the center of her arthritic hand. Mama Gene stared at the orbs in the harshness of the overhead light. Their mass dissected the length of her lifeline. She had been told by a storekeeper when she was a young girl that she would have a long life. The salmon colored line arched strong and deep between her thumb and index finger, extending to the edge of her hand and seemingly beyond. She remembered feeling happy when the woman told her that. She had always thought that a long life was the same as a good one. She had been wrong so many times. All she had left were clothes and the worn spot on the couch that smelled of Old Spice and Murray's like the back of his head. No one should have expected her to stay. She was an old woman now. An old woman who loved an old fool more than she ever thought to show him. Her dying would be his pyre. Her pills would be the salvation she gave into completely for once, and God would have to make room.

Chapter Forty

First time Selah mentioned Parker's name around Peter it felt like a sin. Not that she wasn't sinning already, but a bigger sin, like the sin of omission was more tasteful because of its silence.

Selah had started to feel strange about always saying *my husband, my husband.* She had to give him his name back because the veil of husband was stealing away her identity of him. He was more than that. Even if Selah had forgotten what he used to be.

"Parker deserves better than me," Selah said out of the blue. She lay on her back with her bare breast blocking part of Peter's face as he lay across her stomach.

"You finally said his name. You must trust me or something."

Selah could tell Peter was smiling, not because he was happy, but because he was tickled.

"Well that's his name," she said with bite. "Parker Lareaux. I've been married to him—let's just say we've been together a while."

"Parker. Sounds like the name of one of those smooth talkers to me."

Selah's Bed

"He's a deacon in the church," Selah pushed the side of Peter's head with her palm.

Peter grabbed her hand and flattened it out on his forehead, his hand atop hers. Her heat melted into his skin.

"Like I said, one of those smooth talking en-tre-po-negroes. 'Yeah, my name's La-row. Leroy Parker SaintJames La-row, and I'm here to puff up my pockets as I puff you full of Jesus. Hold on to your purse when you fall out in the spirit 'cause whatever falls on the sanctuary floor is mine.' "

Peter didn't know Parker at all. Anyone who knew Parker remotely knew that he was sold out for God. She just listened.

"And you know, deacons are the sneakiest in the line of 'um. It's like mid-level management—a little power, but not enough; they'll steal you blind."

Selah attempted to push his head again, but he blocked her hand.

"Where's he go?"

"Mount Calvary, but he's studying to be a minister."

"You act like you love him."

Selah lifted her head.

"Why did you ask me that?"

Peter played with Selah's hand. "I didn't ask you nothing. You've been talking about the man a lot lately."

"Is that a problem, Peter?"

"No, I can roll with it." Peter kissed the center of Selah's palm. She wanted to wipe it away.

"Are you sure?" she asked.

Peter didn't answer.

Chapter Forty-One

April 2, 1978

He says he doesn't want you right now and I know he doesn't understand what he is saying. He thinks we will be able to have other children when we are ready. But there is just one you. Just one Michelle, and another child will not be you. When I asked him what I was supposed to do, he just looked at me with his head cocked like I was stupid and turned away. I didn't turn away though. No matter how much silence overran the moment.

I keep thinking about Abraham. How he almost sacrificed his son in the land of Moriah. How Isaac was bound by his father on a stack of wood. I don't understand. I've thought about it a thousand times and I just don't understand how he could think to do it—even though God told him so. I shouldn't think about such things, but I do. Maybe it's just a product of you having a young mommy. But my mother was young when she had me, and so was Mama Gene when she birthed her. This is my tradition. It won't be yours though. You will be married and God will answer you when you call.

Chapter Forty-Two

She already knew she was pregnant; this visit wasn't about that. This visit was to prove Selah unsuitable. That's why Mama Gene chased after her like a heavy shadow all morning. Selah hadn't gotten the chance to clasp her bra in peace before Mama Gene knocked for the second time.

"You have thirty minutes," she shouted through the door.

"I'll be out when I'm ready," Selah said, with enough edge in her voice to get the hell knocked out of her on any other day.

Mama Gene didn't even acknowledge the bite. She spoke more calmly than normal. "I wrapped you up an egg burrito in tin foil and left it on the stove to take with you."

Selah glared at the closed door. She didn't want her funky burrito, even if the smell of cooked eggs and iron skillets weren't making her nauseous. Selah put her hand over her mouth and tried not to gag. Runny, nasty, metal-tasting eggs. Chicken baby flesh. She swallowed. Mama Gene had set the appointment for Selah herself, told her to look nice and respectable. Selah knew what her grandmother meant, *Don't make me look any worse than I already do.* Selah slipped on an almost clean white T-shirt, a pair of faded red shorts, and rainbow flip-flops. Her hair was hand brushed into a rough, balled up pony-tail and her feet were not oiled. She got back in bed and let her legs hang off the edge at the knees. She would lie there until Mama Gene knocked for the third time. Selah wasn't going to make this easy for Mama Gene. Selah wanted her baby and no counselor presenting teenage pregnancy options was going to change her disposition.

She would be twenty in less than a year, that had to mean some-thing. She was basically an adult, no matter what Mama Gene thought. Besides, Selah had waited past most the girls in her neighborhood any-way. Frieda Perkins's daughter Anne was on her second. Tina had a lit-tle boy named Anthony James and though Tasha-Marie didn't have any children to speak of, everyone knew she'd gotten pregnant four times before she'd even started the twelfth grade. Mama Gene should have been proud of Selah. She should have been proud that she was about to become a grandmother for the second time. But all Mama Gene did was turn up her lip and drive Selah into the dirt. "I've done al-ready raised my daughter, and my granddaughter. I ain't about to have another hungry crumb snatcher up in my house. Nuh uh, no I'm not, *shhhit.* You trying to eat me out of the projects. I ain't gone be home-less over no nappy-headed child I didn't have no fun making."

Selah could look at Mama Gene and see the nastiness forming be-hind her eyes. All this made Selah long for her real momma. Ruthie Mae might have been happy to have a grandchild. Selah lay atop the sheets and shook her head unconsciously. Selah didn't know what Ruthie Mae would have done. In her gut she knew that Ruthie was still trying to live the life of a twenty-year-old herself. So when Mama Gene knocked, she would go to this appointment because Mama Gene was the only ground she had to walk on.

Chapter Forty-Three

She realized that she had never been in Mama Gene's house by her-self. It seemed like Mama Gene or Papa Frank was always there or just around the corner so that if Selah screamed real loud she would reach them.

Selah sat alone in her childhood space. The pea-green room would forever be green, no matter how many times someone would paint over its walls after Mama Gene's things were long gone. Memories would always be here; it was the place they were born in. Selah sat on what used to be her bed. It was small and stale, and time had taken over its possibility. The room had become a utility room for Mama Gene. The linoleum was covered with thin areas of dirt that would have moved easily years ago with the slightest touch of broom or bleach. Now the dirt formed uneven patches that shaded the speckled floor, especially in the small walkway between the bed and the opposite wall. Mama Gene would have whipped Selah's backside twice for having a floor this caked up. She would have made Selah pour Pine-Sol and bleach with the tiniest bit of Comet into the yellow mop bucket, knee-wash the floor with a boar-bristled brush, then towel it dry so that no tinge of green or grit was present.

Mama Gene should whoop me now, Selah thought amidst the unorganized room of broken-down appliances and jumbled boxes shapeshifting in its corners. She should whip Selah because Selah should have done more than this to protect Mama Gene. She should have known that Mama Gene knew the bus routes to almost every pharmacy in the city. She should have known that Frieda Perkins charged Mama Gene three dollars apiece for her pill of choice. Selah should have realized what had happened to the television in the bedroom and the vacuum cleaner. But that's what happens when you get tired, you let go of responsibilities and hope that they will float away like a red party balloon instead of wallowing tired and dying on the speckled floor in front of you.

Selah let the blue and white heels on her feet drop to the floor. She pushed back on her arms, sliding toward the wall on the coattail of her jacket. She had long since outgrown this place, but there was nowhere more familiar to her in this moment. Selah had become a woman here. Chased away images of Tonio and what her first time should have been like. Mama Gene had cornrowed her hair in this space and Selah had slept with a clean pair of cotton panties on her head to keep the braids in place at night. She had cursed and lied and put on makeup in this room. Cried for the loss of her daughter here.

Selah was sad to be leaving this place for what she thought would be for good this time. After Mama Gene's living room and bedroom furniture were put in storage, all that would remain would be the memories, ones that spilled over ripe into her presence, that were too heavy to take with her all at once.

Chapter Forty-Four

It was weeks later before Peter told her he was married. It wasn't anything she had asked him or anything she wanted to know. He said it like he knew it would bother her and it did. It did because he volunteered it like clothes you take down to the Salvation Army when you are through with them. Peter should have kept his clothes. Selah didn't want to smell another woman's scent on his memory.

"It's the way you kiss. All greedy like. That's how I knew you weren't married, Selah. You may have a husband, but you're not any more married than I am to my wife. That certificate and splitting bills don't make it real."

"Why are you judging me, Peter?" Selah rolled her neck inadvertently.

"I'm not judging you, baby; I'm just making an observation."

"You don't know what I've been through to get me here—so just leave it alone, all right."

Peter smiled. "Did I strike a nerve? I was just messing with you gurrrl."

Selah cut her eyes at him. "Well don't *mess* with me about that. My past is not to be tampered with, okay?"

"Baby, everybody gotta past and everybody's been hurt. I'm not trying to put a value on your hurt; I'm just saying that I knew you - weren't married. I have three kids and a wife. I could lie, but I ain't a husband or a father."

Selah placed her hand on her hip. "Are you bragging? I'll have you know that I am a happily married woman. Thank you very much."

"Okay," Peter said, "whatever salts your pork."

Selah rolled onto her knees and got up for the blanket. Her studio was always closed on Monday, Tuesday, Wednesday, and Thursday. Instead of getting mad at Peter, she found herself thinking that she should open the gallery up on those days as well. The undercurrent was that she knew this thing with Peter couldn't last. She'd been through the same thing with other lovers. She already had a husband. She wasn't going to let Peter break her down past the comfort of sex. That's why he came every Tuesday morning—because he wanted Wednesday, Thursday, and Friday.

Selah couldn't figure out why he wanted her. She was a broken type of woman no matter how much makeup she wore and how many slits she put in her dress. She was beautiful, she felt beautiful, but in the way that shards of colored glass make pretty collages. And no matter how much they argued peacefully and missed each other while their bodies touched at night, Parker Lareaux loved Selah in the way her kind of woman could be loved. From a distance.

Peter wasn't about distance. He wanted the proximity of commitment and routine no matter how much his Tuesday appearances and lack of phone calls during the week lied about it. He was going to try to take her from herself from the inside out. Moment by moment until they had become the only photograph they needed to identify love.

Selah got up from the blanket and Peter pulled her back down again by the swamp of his mouth by biting the back of her ankle then sucking the sweet flesh. Selah was right. Peter did like big women. His momma must have been one—or his first love—because he consumed her body wholly like it was never enough. Made her feel like she needed to eat more with the idea that one day she would be too much. But she would never be too much for Peter. He would stretch his stomach like a boa constrictor if he had to. Peter Couday was so much bigger than she understood. And she fell back down to the blanket in his need for her.

Chapter Forty-Five

April 14, 1978

This may sound strange coming from me, but I was not a virgin when I met your father. I do not want you to think that I am a bad woman or that sex is all I think about. But you must understand my past and know that it was more than sex that drew me to your dad.

Most days I feel heavy. Like a peach tree with fruit that won't drop. Like I imagine grown women feel lugging their complicated days around behind them. But I am mostly a girl, Michelle. And as a girl, I have experienced things that girls shouldn't know. Like sitting on Ms. Perkins's manfriend's lap and feeling a hardness that was familiar. I have let boys touch me and do things I shouldn't let them do. It is not because I am curious, or because Mama Gene didn't raise me right. It is not because it feels so good either. It is because they were men—even as boys, they were men to me, and maybe even the slightest bit like my own father when he was their age. I do not know my father. I don't really know my mother, ei-

ther, to be completely honest. But she is pretty though and men like her a lot. Her laugh is short and loud like, I don't know, firecracker spark. It's there one second and then it is gone, but you remember it being bright when you think about it, even though it leaves gray dust behind.

I want that kind of laugh someday. I don't want to worry the way that I do and think about things too big for me. Sometimes when I lie in bed with my hands on my stomach trying to feel you, I think about my father. I wonder if he knows he is mine. Not if he knows he is mine in the way that I exist, but if he knows that he belongs to me. "My father," that's what that means, ownership. I want to own him, but I don't think that I do. I want rights to his life the way that some kids can walk into their parents' bedroom at night without knocking and jump in bed between them when they are scared. I'm too big to do that now, but I still get scared. From everything Ruthie Mae said about him the one time I asked, I don't think he even wants me to know his name. But I do know his name. Sampton. I - don't know if that is his first name or last but Mama Gene always follows it up quickly with son of a bitch.

Your father is not like that, Michelle. He is a kind person. He kisses my hand and all of my fingers; reads Jayne Cortez poems to me under the bleachers even though his track buddies would think it is uncool. He even read me this "Double Clutch Lover" poem once by Eugene B. Redmond then followed it up with Kamau Daa'ood and Songs of Solomon from the Bible. He is a good man, Michelle. Even though he won't talk to me right now.

I have called and called. I have hung up and called back again minutes later. He does not answer. His mother sneers through the phone and tells me that he is not there. I don't leave messages even though I know our time is running out. Mama Gene says that he must marry me. But how do you marry someone who won't even talk to you? We need more time, Michelle— all of us. But in my heart, I know he will come around. He has to.

Chapter Forty-Six

Mama Gene sat at the bus stop on the north side of Baseline with her hair curled under like a mushroom around her forehead. Her face was shiny, so were her arms and elbows. Selah stared at her grandmother in the side of her eye. She looked like a three-year-old caught in the Vaseline jar. It was Oil of Olay. Selah knew this by the quality of the sheen. It sickened Selah that Mama Gene dressed up for a meeting to kill her baby. It was *her* baby. Selah hadn't figured out how, she loved Mama Gene so much, but she would learn to hate her for this.

Selah slouched on the opposite end of the uncovered metal bench with the foil-wrapped egg burrito sitting between them. Her size ten feet were white like sparsely powdered wedding cookies with bits of brown showing through. Selah chuckled under her breath. She was glad she had ashy feet. She crossed her long, meaty legs out in front of her and showcased her feet for passers-by like some folks do their breasts. *I should have worn a wrinkled shirt from the hamper,* she thought as the sun planted its focus on her skin. Selah raised her hand over her face to shield her eyes.

"You're gonna be hungry if you don't eat," Mama Gene said, not bothering to look down at the burrito.

"I'll throw up," Selah said, not bothering to look at Mama Gene.

"Better to have something in your stomach than nothing."

"If something is better than nothing then why can't I keep my baby?"

Mama Gene held the same arm over arm stance she'd had since - she'd sat down fifteen minutes before.

"I can't afford it, Selah, ain't nothing else I can tell you."

"I can take care of my own baby." Selah sat up straight to plead her case.

Mama Gene took the *Jet* magazine with Lawrence Hilton-Jacobs on the cover from under her arm and started to fan herself in irritation.

"You don't even buy your own Kotex, Selah, how are you gonna raise a chile?"

"I can go back to my job at the drive-in or get another job somewhere." Selah leaned forward, her knees meeting her rounding stomach, and tried to coax Mama Gene's eyes with the intensity of her stare.

"Unh, unh," Mama Gene said, focusing her eyes on the slanted tail of a Buick Deuce and a Quarter waiting at the light. "And them folks gonna let a pregnant black girl serve other kids pizza. *Ummph.*"

Selah looked down at the rainbow flip-flops on her feet and smacked her lips. "Well," she smacked her lips again, "I can just get on welfare like everybody else." She didn't see the slap coming. But when it landed, the heated sweat of Mama Gene's palm came with it. Selah's instinct was to grab the side of her face with both hands.

Instead, she balled her fist in the leg of her shorts as her eyes started to water and the stinging pulsed through her cheek.

"I ain't eat'n that burrito," she said with the dregs of her voice. Her flip-flops became a whirl of spongy color as she tried to focus through the tears.

Mama Gene restacked her arms under her breasts and looked at Selah directly for the first time in weeks.

"Haven't you learned nothin'?" she said through her teeth, her eyes piercing and bloodshot like Selah's. "Why do you think I used to take you to the County? Why do you think I work so hard for you? - Don't break my heart, girl."

Mama Gene turned back around and left Selah to choke on the force of her words. Selah hated for her grandmother to cry. But this was her baby. *This was her baby.* She had already named her. *Michelle.* She even knew what she was going to look like. You can't ask that of someone and expect everything to just be all right. Even if you love them.

Chapter Forty-Seven

Nothing can prepare you to bathe your mother. There is no class you can take, no prayer you can pray that can make you ready for the changing of the guard. Mama Gene had washed Selah in her kitchen sink as a baby while she soaked greens on one side of the sink and baked cornbread with cracklin bits in the old Hardwick oven. She had tended to Selah when she got the runs and changed green shit over and over and over again. Someone should have told Selah that one day it would be her turn. Someone should have made her pay attention to the time it took to turn intention into action.

The first time was the hardest. Selah had learned how to hoist Mama Gene onto the bed using a half folded blanket, place Mama Gene on the center, then pull the blanket up, down, or sideways to adjust Mama Gene's position on the full-size bed. She had mastered the five-minute walk down the three-foot-long hallway to the bathroom. She would hold Mama Gene's arm and waist, then wait for her to muster the energy for each step. Selah had learned to wrap the Scott tissue tight around her fingers and wipe the heavy liquid from between Mama Gene's thighs and that to never fall asleep, without taking Mama Gene to the bathroom first. She'd mastered all of that. But there was something about pulling Mama Gene's panties down her legs to wash her. Something about seeing the plusness of her body uncovered and sacred. Helpless. Selah didn't like this feeling. And Mama Gene being a nurse made it that much more uncomfortable. Mama Gene was ashamed of the sharing between them. Selah could see it in Mama Gene's eyes, the way she looked at Selah, watching her expression for looks of disdain.

"I don't want you to hate me," Mama Gene said, the first time Selah laid Mama Gene flat over two towels on the bed. "I don't want you to feel sorry for yourself because I put you in this situation."

"Don't worry about that, Mama Gene. Just rest, Momma."

Selah couldn't talk; she needed to concentrate. She stuck the washcloth into the Tupperware. The heated purple bowl was warm against her leg. She took the bar of Ivory from the soap dish on the edge of the bed. Circled the towel around the soap, absorbing the soap mush from the flowered tray. Selah closed her eyes and remembered how Mama Gene used to do it.

Place the entire towel over the face. Wipe. Rinse. Check for crystals in the corner of the eyes.

"Is that too warm, Momma?"

"Naw."

Selah sculpted the inside of Mama Gene's ears, taking her towel-covered pinky finger around each fold. She flipped the lobe to clean away the fragile thin brown line of dirt in the crevice.

As Selah re-soaked the cloth, she looked at Mama Gene. She wondered if this is what she would look like in her seventies, but more than anything, she wondered if this is how she would be.

Deflated brown breasts are a blessing, Selah thought. They do not expect to be sucked and coddled like their younger counterparts. Deflated breasts do not expect to be acknowledged every time they walk into a room. They can go hidden behind high-cut clothing and ignored by their owners for weeks at a time, even during bathing. Yes, Selah decided, she would wait for the sagging deflation of her own breasts in anticipation. That might change her. And even change from the outside in, and not the other way around, was better than nothing.

Selah lifted Mama Gene's right breast in her right hand, and sponged with her left into the smooth undervalley of her skin. The feeling surprised her. Mama Gene's breasts were still heavy with milk. Maybe the milk was dried up, maybe it had rotted on the inside, but it was there, and they still wanted to be touched to be beautiful.

Her stomach was wide with polyps of cottage cheese visible in random spots under the skin. Flaccid rolls started heavy around her ribs and lightened into ripples below her waist. Selah breathed in silently through her nose. She was unaware of Mama Gene's monitoring gaze. She let out the breath and for a full moment fixed her eyes on the lazy smile under Mama Gene's belly. It was a Raggedy Ann C-section scar. Patchworked and ridged over into an over-present memory on her flesh. Selah held the wash towel to her gowned stomach; it left a gray circle of wetness that stuck to Selah's skin as she got into bed that night.

Selah was not supposed to know these things yet. She was not supposed to know that milk needs touch and that the body could be a battleground of stretches and striations. She was not supposed to know that Mama Gene's breasts sagged two inches above her navel and that there were seven light brown ridges etched into the skin of both breasts. She should not have known about the gray tufts of hair and the Preparation H. She wanted to go back to how things were before. She wanted to kick herself for not enjoying the good stuff, like scratching the white lines in Mama Gene's scalp and picking the hard skin from the bottom of her feet.

Chapter Forty-Eight

Peter Couday said things with his eyes that his words only captured a glimpse of. It was the way that he cut and pasted Selah, piecing her together moment by moment until she could see herself in the blue-green orbs of his eyes. Selah would find him looking at her the same way that Mama Gene inspected her crossword puzzles—diligently and waiting. He'd lay on his back as Selah reviewed proofs, his head tilted sideways, his eyes following her eyes as she scrolled with a magnifying glass down the page. He was never playful in these moments. He didn't crack jokes or allow himself to be tickled by information that clanked lead-like in his ears. He just watched, never smiling back when Selah smiled at him to bridge the distance. Peter knew that smiles could be given to friends and enemies; Peter wanted something of substance.

Selah dropped the proofs to the floor and stretched her arms over her head to relieve her back.

"You want to hear the silliest thing?" She smiled again.

Peter kept his hands parked behind his head, still studying her. His Choctaw high cheekbones arched a heavy yawn against his skin when he spoke.

"No."

Selah smiled to herself, feeling the full rumble of his solitary word. She bent at the waist and stretched her arms across her knees.

"I understand if you are not feeling well today, Peter, but really, you can feel free to go home any time you like. It's not like we're committed or anything." Selah's voice was soft and licorice sweet.

Peter circled her with his eyes once more. "I'm fine, Selah Wells."

Selah looked at Peter as he looked at her. He should have smiled at her by now, she thought. He should have grabbed her under her breast and sucked her tongue back into his mouth for round three. He wanted something, and Selah didn't like the way he was trying to get it.

"You know what, Peter, it's time for you to go."

"What's really wrong with you, Selah?"

Selah slapped her hands to her knees. "Where did that come from? Is this inspect the goods day? You know, Peter," she spoke slowly, "just go."

Peter glanced over at the clock and began to speak.

"I think you need to be honest with yourself. You—"

"Really Park—Peter, don't start this."

"Oh, so I'm Parker now? Who was I fifteen minutes ago when we were making love?"

"We don't make love, Peter, we have sex," she paused. "You know what, to be honest with you, we don't even do that, we fuck." Selah shook her head. "What do you want me to say?"

"I want to know what you want from me." Peter stared at her as he grabbed his boxers from the folded pile of clothing on the floor.

As painful as this moment was, she saw beauty in him. Selah wanted to capture it. This was the most fully human and exposed she had ever seen him before.

"I want what we have, Peter," she said.

"And what is that, Selah?"

"We just play. Somewhere between the moon and the morning on Tuesdays."

Chapter Forty-Nine

The bus was crowded with a special kind of funk that happens when ghetto elements and heat meet. The noonday desert sun and sour armpits incubated the potency. Had Selah been alone she would have sat in the back of the bus, behind the second door so that she could feel the rush of wind each time it opened and closed. Instead, Mama Gene chose the first available seats behind the bus driver. Selah squeezed past her grandmother's knees and sat in the concave blue seat. Mama Gene's damp, oily arm rested atop her own. Selah leaned away.

Small rectangular portals opened inward near the bus's dome, though the large square windows that surrounded the bus were sealed closed. Selah stared hard out of the window, even when she - wasn't looking at anything. The bus cruised in the gutter lane for spurts and stopped every time the white cord was pulled. As chalky lines dried on her face, they were replenished promptly by new tears. Seeping tears, birthed without the luxury of sound.

Selah's Bed

"Next stop Baseline and Arrowhead."

The driver was barely audible. A short Latino woman behind Selah grazed the nub of her ponytail with her grocery bag.

"*Lo seinto*," she said, as she moved quickly from her seat toward the front exit. Selah didn't move and she didn't wipe the lines from her face that bled over the rise of her lip into her mouth. To wipe would mean that she was apologetic or ashamed of her tears. Mama Gene would have to wipe them herself if she didn't want to be embarrassed. She would have to take Selah aside like a toddler and swab away the snot forming around the circles of her nose. What more could Selah do to show that this wasn't right? She didn't want a meeting. She didn't want options. Her choice was growing in the lining of her womb.

The world moved by in slow motion as Selah's forehead rested on the simulated glass. *ABORT,* she thought to herself as she peered into an abandoned lot. Industry had already started to be pulled from Baseline Avenue, just like other parts of the city. Bob's Big Boy had closed, so had Alpha Beta grocery store. *ABORT,* Selah thought again and opened her eyes wider in concentration. After *aardvark, abacus, abandon.* She couldn't think of any other words that came before it in the dictionary. Selah unpinned her arm from under her grandmother's fleshy elbow and placed it on the small swell of her stomach. *ABORT.* She knew what it meant. Her forehead frowned as the words formed on her salty tongue. *TO STOP. TO MAKE GO AWAY. TO LIE.*

Her entire life was within walking distance of this moment. Tonio, Richard, the touches. And that's when Selah remembered. She didn't have to stay. She didn't have to mourn something that - couldn't happen if she wasn't there. It was easy to break away. She would pull out of the eyes first. Drain the energy from her tear ducts, back through her sockets into her womb. She and Michelle would be safe there. They could be company for each other. As Selah pulled herself inward, her lips were the last parts to follow. The smile was real. She had never gone into her private space with some-one else before.

Chapter Fifty

She wanted to cry, but couldn't. For everything that would go wrong during their visit. For every non-remembrance and miss-called name. Selah would sit in her car, the windows rolled up into the black rubber seal, music coating her delirium. It was always Tina Turner's "Simply the Best" she listened to. She needed the reassurance of someone who had been through something—and Tina had been through something, a singing teeny-bopper couldn't quiet the scared woman inside of her. Selah mouthed the words, saliva gathering in the corners of her lips. *Simp-ly the best, bet-tah than all the rest . . .* She sung hard to herself, eyes closed tight, fear rolling her voice off beat.

She did this once a week now, twice a week when she found some extra strength. The sadness of her loss always overtook Selah as she sat parked outside of Sweet Day Convalescent Home. Despite the crocheted welcomings on the door, the pictures of smiling seniors on the walls in thick wood frames, the happy colored furniture in the reception area, this was not a happy place. This was the end of living.

The end of making major choices for yourself and coming and going as you please. This was a place of forced medicine and nine o'clock lights-out. A place of tired nurse-patient interactions and volunteer visits by strangers kinder than family.

Her goal had been to visit every day. The rest home was on Slauson near Western Avenue, less than fifteen back-street minutes from her front door. Selah had done that initially, visited Mama Gene every single day at lunchtime. They'd sit at the small round table in Mama Gene's room, Selah eating the last of the roast beef between two slices of bread, her grandmother drinking apple juice from a small white box and complaining that the Salisbury steak was dry with too little seasoning.

"And they didn't give me my Hershey's chocolate, Selah. They're supposed to give me one bar every day, Selah, like you said, but -

they're not giving it to me, Selah, they're eating it themselves, Selah."

Mama Gene looked at Selah. Her face frowned up in confusion as to how the nurses could be so mean and unloving toward her. "These are stingy women, Selah, mean, ornery old heifers with no kind of heart." Mama Gene's lips puckered into a tight brown fist and her words started to hit hard in Selah's ears. "I-don't-know-why-you-make-me-live-here-with-these—these peo-ple." With the back of her wrinkled hand, Mama Gene ever so lightly knocked the white apple juice box off the edge of her tray onto the white-tiled floor. Selah looked at Mama Gene, teeth clinched inside her locked jaw, her face yielding no expression. Apple juice trickled into the gray grout lines separating the tiles.

Mama Gene folded her hands in the lap of her skirt and sat quietly staring back at Selah. Tight black orbs loosened into bland knots. The whites of Mama Gene's eyes were dry just like Selah's.

Selah's Bed

Selah didn't quite understand how a six foot ton of a woman could shrink into a worn-down prune. Mama Gene had been Selah's mountain. She had always felt safe growing up in Mama Gene's house. She was loved and fed and wanted.

"I'll have a nurse clean that up, Mama Gene." She grabbed her grandmother's hand in hers and squeezed. "And I'll make sure those ornery nurses stop eating your candy bars. Those women don't know who they are messin' with. Mama Gene's granddaughter ain't gonna stand for no acting out."

She kissed both of her grandmother's hands and held them to the outside of her face.

"Now, I'm gonna see you tomorrow, Mama Gene. You eat the rest of your food and I'll bring a small baggy of Lawry's seasoning salt tomorrow for us to fix the meat up if it doesn't taste right, okay? Tomorrow, Momma."

Selah walked back to her car smiling. This was a good visit. Mama Gene had remembered Selah's name.

Chapter Fifty-One

Peter knew that this wasn't how a woman looked when she'd gotten left outside in a storm. Selah had rearranged the furniture behind her eyes. Backboarded her soul so that want and regret couldn't seep through. And she smiled, holding on to spaces that had long ago gotten too big to be hers.

Some pain becomes its own entity; it can no longer be stuffed behind loose eyeballs, like balled-up paper, to hold them in their sockets.

Sometimes pain lets go of you first. Even when holding on to it is all that you know.

This is the scary part, when you miss the weight of your luggage but you still have proof of your journey. Peter had already been through the disrobing process and adjusted to all the men he would never be—a husband, a father, a provider. Whole. Just like his own father, Peter had given empty spaces like chewed-up gifts to people who should have been more important to him, pockmarking time with his absence. But if he couldn't be whole, he still wanted to love her.

And he did love her, in all the ways that he could. In the way that travelers love. Incrementally, occupying spaces that they may not have anger, greed, or hope enough to occupy tomorrow. Tuesday morning had become his church. And Selah was the almost warm vessel he housed himself in.

It wasn't permanent. But Peter felt better here, better than he did anywhere else. So did Selah. Even when they didn't get along and their reflections clashed hard against a reality they wished was so different. They could comfort each other, because they'd both been stripped down of true wanting. They did comfort each other, even if the solace wore off in the taking.

Chapter Fifty-Two

Selah showed up with seasoning salt. Not the next day as she had promised Mama Gene, but four days later. Each visit loaded her constitution with knowing, because each time she walked through Sweet Home's glass doors she understood a little more what the smell pulsing through its halls meant. She should have gone the day before; she should have stayed longer on her last visit or taken Mama Gene to Baskin-Robbins for Marble Fudge in a sugar cone during the weekend. But the littlest things required so much more energy for Selah than they did in her twenties, thirties even. Selah was split by Mama Gene's Alzheimer's as much or more than Mama Gene was. She knew this because though it was Mama Gene losing pieces of her life, it was Selah who had to stand witness as Mama Gene slipped away into somewhere else.

Selah stopped at the nurses' station and sat the Ziploc baggie of seasoning salt, onion powder, and garlic salt on the counter atop the Sweet Home information pamphlets laid out fan style. The baggie was filled with Mama Gene's Special Blend. She used this mix every time she baked, boiled, or fried chicken, pork chops, cube steak, catfish—anything. Selah used to observe Mama Gene in the narrow kitchen, her body taking up most of the aisle, the apron strings tied tight, creating definition in her waist. She always cooked in a pale pink linen housecoat with twelve pearlized snaps down the center. As a little girl, Selah would position herself in the middle of the kitchen doorway with her coloring book and Crayolas. She liked to watch Mama Gene. And every time she did, the oversize orange container with the Lawry's label peeled off sat next to her cutting board.

Mama Gene would take the chicken defrosting in the sink out of the brown and yellow plastic bag and wash it whole. Then she'd hold the chicken by one leg for leverage and section it into pieces. After Mama Gene spaced the pieces on the cutting board, she'd sprinkle the seasoning mix evenly over every section then flip them over and do the other side. She even added seasoning to the flour to make up for any seasoning that was lost as it tossed in the paper bag, then she fried the chicken with a big white scoop of Crisco.

"May I help you?" A nurse walked behind the counter and leaned forward projecting her small voice toward Selah.

"Hi. I'm Selah Wells, Eugenia Wells's granddaughter—"

"I'm pretty sure she's ready for visitors." She slid a pen down the list on the clipboard in front of her and stopped the ballpoint on Mama Gene's name. "Yes, she's all set; you're welcome to go on in." She smiled.

Selah smiled back. "Thank you, Miss . . ." she read the woman's badge, "Miss Estrell. May I ask you a quick question?"

"Sure," she said, her voice getting even lower.

Selah matched her voice. "I just want to clarify something. I was speaking with my grandmother a few days ago and she said that the nursing staff wasn't giving her the Hershey bars I left for her; she's supposed to get one bar every day. Would you be able to tell me if - she's getting them or not?"

"Well," she paused to a whisper, "let me check her file and see what I can find out. I'll be back in a few moments." She disappeared into the back office door she had appeared from when Selah first arrived.

Selah leaned on the counter and looked through one of the pamphlets as she waited. It was the same pamphlet that had helped her decide that Sweet Home would be a good place for Mama Gene. Everyone looked happy in this pamphlet. The front flap featured a forty-something lady and a child smiling and hugging a gray-haired woman in a wheelchair. The second page showed two seniors playing cards in the activity room. The third page showcased an older man sitting on the examining table as he looked intently at the doctor, who had a stethoscope around his neck and one hand on the older - man's shoulder. Care, camaraderie, family, and safety. That's why Selah had brought her here. She wanted Mama Gene to be safe; she - didn't want to worry anymore. But she did worry, maybe even more now than she had when Mama Gene lived with her and Parker in their home.

"Yes, Ms. Wells," the nurse smiled; a look of concern overtook her face. "I spoke to the charge nurse and looked over your grandmother's chart. The daily meal plan shows that your grandmother has been receiving her candy bars every evening at dinner in place of tapioca or chocolate pudding. I checked her cubby hole and there are still six bars left before she runs out."

"Like I said, I just wanted to clarify. My grandmother was really upset the last time I came and I—thank you." Selah placed the pam-

phlet back into the stack and turned toward Mama Gene's room
with the baggie in hand.

"Ms. Wells, please always feel free to ask us anything you need to,
any time. We realize that these types of changes are as difficult for
the family as they are for the patient. And know that Alzheimer's, because of the deterioration of memory, can make little things even
that much more difficult. Rarely have I found that a patient is trying
to cause havoc; your grandmother honestly may not remember that
she ate the candy bars. Memory can fail from one moment to the
next. And believe me when I say that patients often make up the
wildest stories—that we not only eat all of their candy bars, but that
we eat their dinners too." She smiled. "It's the nature of the disease."

"What about the stories? Sometimes she sees monkeys in the
room or says she's other people."

The nurse shrugged her shoulders. "I'm not really sure why that
is, Ms. Wells. Looking over your grandmother's chart, it might be
delirium caused by the long-term combination drug use. It could be
another acute condition I'm not aware of, you would have to ask her
doctor. I can arrange a phone meeting if you like."

Selah shook her head. "I've already spoken to her doctors and I
was told basically the same thing. Thank you."

Selah turned from the counter and proceeded to walk down the
wide hall. The rubber soles of her tennis shoes made suctioning
sounds as she walked. This was always the worst part of her arrival,
walking past the wrinkled bodies slouched into wheelchairs. Men
and women, some partially dressed with button-down sweaters or
blankets atop their gowns sat still in the doorways of their rooms.
One bald man with liver spots on his face and hands sat in the middle
of the hallway. They were waiting for something, but Selah knew it -
wasn't family or friends. It was strange to Selah that the convales-

cent home always seemed more devoid of visitors than the cemetery. They had no one to comb their hair with care or to wipe the slobber dripping from their mouths. Selah couldn't think about the other patients too much. She was there to see Mama Gene and that was always hard enough.

Mama Gene was sitting in bed when Selah walked in. She didn't acknowledge Selah. She didn't smile or give the slightest clue that she realized that Selah was in the room with her. Selah shuffled past the railed bed and sat down at the small table with her handbag over her jean covered legs.

"Good evening, Mama Gene."

Two pillows were propped behind Mama Gene's head and the mattress was raised into a sitting position. Mama Gene looked at the stark white wall in front of her; the television anchored to it was turned off. She stared intently at the wall.

"Ahhhh," Mama Gene said, her body slumping a little farther down in the bed, her shoulders rounding forward.

The *Ahhhh* was to herself, not Selah.

"Are you ignoring me today, Mama Gene?"

"I don't like that name."

"Mama Gene?"

Mama Gene ran the back of her thumb over the paint-chipped fingernails on the opposite hand.

"No. I don't like that name. That name is a homely, mammie kind of a name and I am not your mammie."

"Oh . . . okay," Selah said, feeling her eyes get large. "That's fair I suppose." She pulled the purse strap over her head and turned away from Mama Gene to place her purse on the table and to hide the change in her expression. In Selah's Alzheimer's and Dementia support group she had been told that changing expressions too quickly

and seeming to be in judgment of the patient could start to under-
mine the patient's dignity over a period of time. Selah didn't want to
do that to her grandmother. She pretended to need some Chap Stick
out of her purse and applied the vanilla balm to her upper and lower
lips. When she was sure her expression was neutral she turned back
around. "What would you like me to call you?"

Mama Gene shrugged her shoulders, seemingly in silent disgust
with herself. She looked down and fingered the purple juice stain on
her hospital gown.

"Don't matter, just not no backwards assed name like Mama
Gene."

Dr. Horim and Dr. Lee had explained to Selah that her grandmother's reactions were most probably the by-product of a partially
reversible dementia caused by the toxic effects of years' dependency
on codeine, diazepam, and muscle relaxants. Selah had explained to
the doctors that Mama Gene had often taken more pills than had
been recommended at one time and that she had often mixed two or
three different pills together to achieve a particular type of "high."

"I'll be honest with you, Ms. Wells, your grandmother may be on
painkillers and muscle relaxants for the rest of her life. She's older,
most older citizens do have some form of legitimate pain. Our goal
here is not to stop your grandmother from taking these medica-
tions, that's what a drug rehabilitation center does, our goal is to
control her intake so that she doesn't abuse them."

Selah hoped in the most twisted of ways that one day she would
be able to consider the disease a blessing. It could be something better than pretending. Mama Gene wouldn't have to pretend because
between the pills and the Alzheimer's, she wouldn't know. She -
wouldn't know that her daughter had disappeared and left her to
raise her granddaughter. She wouldn't know that Ruthie Mae was

just following in her bastard father's footsteps and that Papa Frank had died a quick hard death. She wouldn't know any of these things, not for real, not the way the rest of us know them when we awake from sleep in the tumor of memory. She would not wake up, because at some point there would be nothing left to remember.

When Mama Gene's attention span grew tired of trying to wipe the grape juice stain away with her bed sheet, she went back to stroking her fingernails again. Selah sat there in the uncomfortable wooden chair. She wasn't close to tears because she couldn't cry. She was close to feeling, though. Feeling the same loss that floated unsanitarily into the room every time she would visit. Selah made a pact with herself. Today, as Mama Gene drifted off into somewhere, she would too. During this visit Selah would call herself Iris. Selah thought about how Iris would brush Mama Gene's hair and oil her scalp with olive oil. Iris would push vanilla oil into the cracked, hard skin on the bottom of Mama Gene's ashy feet. Iris would soon sit laughing at Mama Gene's bedside telling her about how she invented the first pressing comb and not Madam C. J. Walker. Only in the broken moments of laughter and hairline silences would Iris fade and Selah remember that she missed sitting in the orange vinyl chair in Mama Gene's kitchen, stove blaring, and the pressing comb leaving the residue of melting oil to run down her scalp.

Chapter Fifty-Three

April 20, 1978

There are some bus rides young girls shouldn't have to take. But Mama Gene says that I should at least know my options. Maybe they are right though. I didn't have a mother, now I am trying to be one. And then I think back to the day I really thought I was pregnant.

I put on white panties to ensure that it came. White, crisp, new panties from Lerner's Department Store that used to be on E Street between Fourth and Fifth, but had moved to the new Central City Mall a few years before. Lerner's always had the right size underwear for bigger girls. Not fat girls, but girls with meat. The panties had a thick cotton crotch, the kind that would make you feel dry down there no matter how humid and hot the weather was. I wore these panties, the ones that I would have never worn on my menstrual cycle because I had paid three dollars for them and three dollars was a lot to spend on one pair of underwear.

I wanted my period to start that badly. Enough to sacrifice my good "draws," as Mama Gene would call them. Any other time I would have worn a good pair of undies without a Kotex pad, I would have gotten permanent stains. Stains that would have never come completely out, just turned lighter shades of brown and yellow with each wash.

This time nothing came. And I prayed, Michelle. I prayed in dreams and on my knees. I prayed like I knew God and we had been close at some point in my life. I wanted cramps. I wanted pains that Midol and the strongest codeine would not have helped go away. I did not want you at first; I wanted blood.

I feel sorry for this now. I wasn't supposed to want Parker enough to sacrifice myself. He was supposed to be just a boy. But he noticed me. Noticed me in the way that Tony Perkins noticed me. And I liked the way it felt. No guy had ever wanted me beyond lust. On the days I didn't work, I would hang out after school with Tasha-Marie or Carla in the bleachers to watch the track team practice. Some might say that Tasha-Marie and Carla were prettier than I was because they were thinner, but not to Parker. He acknowledged them out of kindness only. He acknowledged me out of desire. I would watch him in his purple running shorts and yellow practice tank "stick and move" with the baton in his right hand. I would pay attention to the muscles in his legs when he jumped the black and white hurdles. He was sexy to me, but kind mostly. Too thin to be a football player or even a good basketball player, but he was agile. Tone and thin.

When he circled the track he would smile at me. Not every single drill, but often enough to keep me watching and waiting. Each time he looked up, he knew exactly where I was, like he had memorized me. Then after practice was over and he had cooled down by jogging the bleachers, he'd come up and sit a few feet away from me. We'd rap. He'd stretch his torso over his left leg, his left arm gripping the tip of his track shoe. I knew he liked me because no one who had any kind of choice would choose to stretch in the bleachers unless someone was drawing him there.

Selah's Bed

Before he ever kissed me, he held me. Parker held me like he was the safest place I would ever know in my life. That's how I fell in love. That's how I lost myself in him. I hate myself for that. For letting a man's arms take away what I already knew. Women have babies by themselves in my neighborhood, just like I would.

On days like today my resistance is worn. I can't find the sheer belief to comprehend how we'll make it through all of this life I have created for us. I am afraid to be your mother. I am afraid that I will be like my mother and leave because to have you look into my eyes would be too painful.

It is not the hard times I am afraid of. I would scrub toilets to keep you. I don't have anything I'll lose by gaining you. But when I settle into myself, when I think long and hard about the possibility of you, I am afraid you will see it. It will be subtle. It will coat the laugh lines in my fingers when I touch you. And under the happiness, under the joy of what I have created, under what is mine and no one else's, when I look at you too long, you will know it's there. A tender hatred. One that you have not earned, but is yours nonetheless. It is the only thing I understand about motherhood. It is the only thing my mother ever gave me.

Chapter Fifty-Four

Selah snatched an old sneaker from under the bed and threw it at the door. When it missed, she got up and slammed the door shut herself. She hated when Mama Gene and Papa Frank argued, mainly because the topic was always the same. Selah laid back down atop the light green comforter she had had since she was seven years old. The cotton squares had flattened, and when she held it up to the light, she could see areas where the batting had torn apart and left the top and bottom covers touching.

No matter how old she got, her body never desensitized to the sound of their voices screaming at each other. When she was pregnant and this happened, she would place a thermal blanket over her stomach so that Michelle couldn't absorb the negative energy. That - didn't matter now. They could scream each other into oblivion if they wanted to as long as Selah didn't have to look at them as they did it.

It had been three months since Michelle. Three months since the open gown and tissue paper against her back. Selah remembered every detail. How her butt fleshed to the end of the pink vinyl table. The light shining hard against the broken butterfly between her legs exposing its folds. Her bare feet in stirrups. The gush of fluid. But what she remembered most was her grandmother. How when she exited the closet-size room with a maternity pad taped between her legs, Mama Gene sat there, barely awake, but smiling. Selah knew what it was. Mama Gene had taken her pills. And instead of her grandmother holding Selah's arm, Selah bent down to lift Mama Gene up and escorted her to the bus stop.

Selah started to think about Mama Gene differently after that. She was just in her fifties, but she was forgetful now and she would say things sometimes that didn't make sense. Every time Selah told Mama Gene that it was the pills that made her act this way, she would deny it.

"When you clean green shit from an old white man's crack and lift patients every day, I might listen to you," she'd rebut. "You don't know what condition my body is in."

Selah didn't need evidence and she didn't need to understand. She heard the small slur in her grandmother's voice after she had taken a few pills too many. When Mama Gene got on her nerves, Selah used to get mad at herself for wishing that Mama Gene *would* take a pill. At least then she would get off her back. But since Michelle, Mama Gene rarely fussed with Selah anymore. She saved all of her angst for Papa Frank, especially when her supply ran out.

Mama Gene didn't start out in a tizzy fit, she would have to work herself into it. She would ask Papa Frank sweet as pie to go pick up her refill from Longs Drugs down the street and sweet as pie Papa Frank would refuse. He knew she was embarrassed to pick them up herself because she went through many—120 of each pill plus two

Jenoyne Adams

to three refills per month. She wouldn't have gotten so many if she -
didn't have two doctors. One doctor for her back, the other for the
numbness and pain in her right leg.

Papa Frank usually just ignored Mama Gene when she tried to
bribe him with smothered pot roast and fried okra or said she -
wouldn't get mad if he stayed out late on Saturday to shoot an extra
game at Walker's Pool Hall. He tried hard to ignored her, but sometimes he'd yell, "If you were on The County, they'd give you those
red stickers and I think that would be the best thing for you."

He'd say it like a threat. But Mama Gene wasn't on The County.
Selah was, but her medical stickers were green. And when she got
into one of her moods, especially when Selah told her that she was
going to keep Michelle, Mama Gene was sure to bring it up.

She'd look Selah in the eyes and say it like she was saying a nasty
word. "The Count-tee," she'd say gutturally, her nostrils flared open
and her lips turned out like they stunk. Mama Gene wanted to make
sure that Selah understood what she was in for for bringing a child
into the world under these conditions.

Mama Gene knew firsthand what Selah had to look forward to.
She used to have to go to the county building every month when
Selah was a child to meet with Selah's caseworker. It was embarrassing to Mama Gene. And for that reason, she always made Selah go
with her on her shame walk up Waterman to Gilbert Street. She
wanted to cement in Selah's head that everything bad started and
ended at the welfare office. "Getting pregnant, drinking alcohol,
being fast, taking drugs, and unemployment, all end you up in the
welfare line . . . ask you momma."

Mama Gene could make Selah feel like a particle of dirt stuck on
dog shit, but especially so when she talked about Selah being pregnant to Papa Frank.

"That's Ruthelen Mae's child," she said, and commenced to explain to Papa Frank that if Selah hadn't gotten pregnant, she - wouldn't have gone through all of those pills so quickly. "Half the time she acts just as backward as her momma. How did she think she could afford to keep that baby? Humph."

When Selah stormed out of the house, she didn't slam the door. She didn't have anything to prove to Mama Gene. Her grandmother had gotten what she wanted.

Selah ended up on the Gate, her hair flat on one side from lying in bed, her legs dangling ashy in wrinkled shorts. The sun stung the pupils of her eyes. Selah had stopped going outside after the doctor's visit. She had stopped doing everything that pulled her out of her room. All she did now was write letters. Longish letters. Scribbled letters. Anything to try and make the feeling go away.

Facing north, she could see the back gate of her old elementary school. Life had seemed so much simpler then. The boxed chocolate milks. The tetherball courts. Selah thought about what Mama Gene had called her: Ruthie Mae's child. Sitting there, on the pink concrete wall, Selah couldn't stop herself from wondering if things would have been different if Ruthie Mae would have stayed around.

As cars drove past, Selah thought about the one time she had spent time with her mother outside of Mama Gene's house. Selah was six and Ruthie Mae had convinced Mama Gene that she was flying straight and would take good care of Selah.

"I got me an apartment, Momma, and a job waitressing at this old folks breakfast spot around the corner from the house. And she is my daughter, Momma. I can take care of her for a couple days."

She told Mama Gene that she was ready to "try" to be a mother. That she wanted to "try it out" for the weekend—Friday, Saturday, and Sunday. Selah was excited. She had never gone anywhere alone with her mother, not even to Thrifty's for a ten-cent ice-cream cone. Mama Gene thought about it and said that since Selah was Ruthie's biological child she would give Ruthie the benefit of the doubt.

Selah remembered sitting on the edge of her bed while Mama Gene packed four pairs of pants, five short-sleeve shirts, a night-gown, and two Holly Hobbie coloring books into a travel case. Ruthie Mae picked Selah up from Mama Gene's house early Friday morning, dropped her off at school, and picked her up that after-noon. She took her to the Golden Arches on E Street for dinner, got Selah two cheeseburgers, a large fry, and a vanilla cone with nuts on top. Mama Gene would have never let Selah get a large fry or order nuts on her ice-cream cone. She would have slapped Selah's hand for dipping french fries in her ice cream and told her that she was letting her hoglike ways get the best of her. Ruthie thought it was cute and dipped some of her fries, too. Selah was glad that Ruthie was her momma. Her real momma. She was young and pretty and she wore short-shorts with pink sparkles running down the sides.

Mama Gene would have never worn something like that. She said only women with half-respect wore stuff like that and needed to get the other half kicked back into them by a good ass whoopin'. Selah liked it though. The skintight blouse and white leather sandals with a big toe loop. She was their own neighborhood Josephine Baker, but finer. Men would smile at Ruthie Mae as she switched past, ten feet tall, minding her own business. When they turned their heads to watch her walk away, all Selah could think about was that she would get her some shoes like that some kind of way, whether Mama Gene bought them or not. Selah wasn't old enough to know then that she would outgrow her momma's fine figure quicker than she developed it. But she still got those shoes. And she would wear them with brazen toe polish and power like her mother did.

After watching the *Dick Van Dyke Show* with Selah that night,

Selah's Bed

Ruthie got antsy. Like how Selah got when she was waiting for Mama Gene to go to sleep so that she could flip the lights back on in her room and try out the makeup she and Tina had stolen from her - mother's dresser. Ruthie was waiting for Selah to go to sleep that same way. Selah lay on her mother's stubby couch with a pink polka-dot pillow under her head that smelled of royal crown and pressing comb like Ruthie's hair. She pretended to be asleep.

What Ruthie Mae didn't tell Mama Gene is that although she had gotten a job, it wasn't at a café. She was a waitress, working late nights at the Velvet Lounge serving cocktails. When Ruthie left the apartment, she snuck out shoeless in coffee brown panty hose and locked the top dead bolt behind her. Ruthie stayed out until morning.

When Selah told Mama Gene the next day what Ruthie had done, Mama Gene paid Frieda Perkins five dollars to give her a ride to her ungrateful daughter's house to pick Selah up.

"Ain't a damn thing wrong with this girl, Momma," Ruthie Mae said. "She's just as fine as she wants to be. Stop sheltering her like she ain't got a damn bit of sense of her own. What? Was she going to burn the house down in the middle of the night? That's my baby, Momma; don't you forget it."

Mama Gene swung her finger and pointed so hard at Ruthie Mae's hungover body slapped across the couch that she couldn't even say anything. Just snatched Selah's arm and dragged her out of the house. Selah sat in the backseat of the station wagon on the ride home watching Mama Gene's head shake side to side. "Lawd knows I didn't raise her like this. Lawd knows I never left her alone like that."

Selah wasn't afraid of being left alone in Ruthie Mae's apartment, not really. She lay there on the couch with the brown and orange knit blanket over her shoulders, sticking her fingers in and out of the holes. Some of the holes were too tight to stick her fingers through, but she pushed them through anyway. Ruthie had left the small light over the stove on, and her place was only a one bedroom, so as long as the only noise Selah heard was the squeaking of the couch when she moved around, Selah knew she was alone. She was about to turn seven. At eight, Mama Gene bought her her first training bra so that her rosebuds wouldn't show through her shirt.

That whole night in Ruthie's house, Selah wondered what it would have been like to live with Ruthie Mae, if Ruthie would have gotten tired of her putting french fries in her ice cream and if she would have spanked her for it eventually. She wondered if it would have always been her sitting next to her mother in the front seat of the worn-out Pacer, or if a man, maybe her father, would have replaced her. But more than anything, as Selah sat on the "Gate," she wondered if Ruthie Mae would have let her keep her baby.

When Selah finally decided to leave the "Gate" to walk back home, the sun was starting to go down. She figured Mama Gene would have gotten her pills by then and would be loaded or knocked out. At least the house would be quiet. Her bedroom would be cooler now. She walked at a casual pace, like she wasn't in a hurry to leave where she was or to get to where she was going. When she rounded the corner from Crest View onto Sycamore, she saw him. She was more than surprised. From the way he never returned her phone calls, no matter how urgent the message she left with his mother, she didn't know if she'd ever see him again. Parker sat on the two-foot wall in front of Mama Gene's apartment with his back erect and his hands locked between his legs. Selah kept her pace. *He has his nerve,* she thought to herself as he sat there staring into the motionless tree in the front yard. At least he should have looked broken. At least he should have looked as bad as she did. But even from a distance, he looked normal and clean, like he had washed his face that morning and sprayed Right Guard under his arms. Selah neared closer to him, remembering how she used to get excited when she saw him across campus. Four months ago she would have tried to fix her hair and straighten her clothes before he noticed her. There was no giddiness now, just an intimate regret made fresher by his presence.

"Why are you here?" Selah said, as she crossed the driveway into the grass.

"I wanted to talk to you; see how you were doing." He looked up at her, wincing as if the sun were directly overhead.

"You shouldn't have come," she said studying him, not caring that the brightness had left his eyes.

"I haven't been seeing you around school," Parker said.

She smirked. "No, you haven't." His shirt was new. *He has the nerve to come to my grandmomma's house in a new shirt. After all I've been through,* she thought. Selah didn't have time for this. She didn't have time for a man who could go shopping at the mall while she was lying on an operating table.

"Umm, how's your grandmother?" he asked.

"Passed out probably—what do you want?" Selah crossed her arms over her chest and walked two steps forward so that her ashy knee touched the wall's edge.

"I wanted to see you."

"*Pleassse.* Save the drama for your momma. I'm going in the house." Selah grabbed the screen door handle, then let it go. "When I needed to talk," she pointed her finger, "you didn't want to talk. I - don't need you now so you can just go hide back under your momma and her Bible."

Parker flipped one leg over the wall so that he faced Selah and gave her a look of irritation.

"Don't make this any harder than it already is, okay."

"*Don't raise* your voice in front of my grandmomma's house and - don't come here, expecting *me* to make a damn thing easy for *you*."

Parker stood up and started to pace in a circle on the grass.

"You think this is easy?" His voice raised higher. "You think it was easy for me to catch the bus over to your grandma's house to see you knowing she probably can't stand me right now?"

Selah just stared. Parker punched the air. "Ugghh. I'm trying to do right, Selah. I don't want things to be like this between us. I even—I've even been going to church and shit. Doesn't that mean something to you?"

"It means you know you're full of it. I poured my heart out to you four months ago. *Four months.* And you're just now getting to my house? Phugggh." Selah blew a puff of air through her barely parted lips.

"You told me you were pregnant, what was I supposed to say? I was scared." He dropped his hands to his legs. "Can't you understand that it took me a second to figure out what I should do?"

Selah leaned back against the wood-framed screen door and shook her head. It was easier not to see him. If she didn't see him, she wouldn't wonder if Michelle would have had his eyes.

"I just," he paused and pounded his chest two times. "I just want you to know that I am trying to change my life. I wasn't living right before and I want to make things different."

"Things *are* different, Parker. You've changed my life enough already."

It took a while for him to speak. Selah stood there expressionless, waiting. Parker raised the right leg of his jeans and stepped over the wall in front of Selah. He reached out to hold the outside of her arms. She tried halfheartedly to shake his hands away.

"Don't hold this against me, Selah. We can work through this."

Selah shook her head no. She wanted to believe him, that he could make everything better, but she was tired of trusting.

Parker rubbed his sweaty hands up and down her forearms.

"I talked to my parents, and they don't agree with me," he paused. "They think I'm too young to get married, but they don't want their grandchild to suffer either."

Selah couldn't believe what she heard. "You late ass mutha-fucka." She pushed the center of his chest full strength with both hands. Parker stepped back to catch his balance.

"Get away from me," she said, never before hearing that kind of shrill in her voice. Selah pulled the screen door open and as she ran into the hall Mama Gene appeared.

"Sshhh. What's wrong, baby?" Mama Gene said with a light, pill-induced slur.

Selah pushed past Mama Gene and ran into her bedroom, her face swollen with heat, her eyes flowing quick tears.

Parker stood in the doorway, wanting to go after her, but knowing not to.

"What else have you gone and done to my grandbaby?"

"Ma'am I—"

"Don't 'Ma'am' me. Your Johnny Come Lately self ain't done nothing but run havoc in Selah's life. Selah was a good girl. She - wasn't gonna end up like me and her momma. You wrunt her."

"Mrs. Wells," Parker spoke low. "I'm trying to make things right by your granddaughter, that's why I came here. I really care for her."

Mama Gene flipped her hand at him and turned around. "Only care you got is 'tween your legs."

"No disrespect, Mrs. Wells, but I really thought about it and I love your granddaughter; I want to marry her."

"Love ain't a thought," Mama Gene spouted as she sat down on the couch.

"May I speak to Selah?"

"Naw, naw. Just take your scrawny self on home. You've talked enough for the day." Mama Gene pointed him to the door.

"No disrespect, but—"

"I'll talk to him, Mama Gene." Selah stood in the darkness of the hall with balled-up tissue in her hand, leaning against the wall.

"The baby's gone, Parker—"

Mama Gene pushed her body up from the couch.

"You do not owe that boy no explanation."

"What do you mean the baby's gone?" Parker searched Selah's shadowed face.

"She means exactly what she said; now get your sorry behind out of my house."

"She's been gone for three months. I waited as long as Mama Gene would let me."

Parker closed his eyes to stop the tears and sandwiched his head between his arms. "Ugghh." He slapped the door, "my baby's gone, Selah?" He punched the wall with his fist, then cowered as tears started to flow freely.

The room stood helpless. Selah cried against the wall. Mama Gene reasoned from behind her veil of pills that Parker really did care for Selah.

Mama Gene grabbed her purse from the end cushion of the couch. "I'm gonna head over to Longs. I trust you two will have my house in one piece when I get back."

They stood across from each other in the quiet, their faces torn, the wave of loss pulsing through the room. There was no make-better-quick remedy for this situation. They would have to start with sorry and work up from there.

Chapter Fifty-Five

Maybe this is just what happens when you are losing someone. The way bitterness rises and eclipses your ability to see clearly. Selah knew that she should have stayed home today. She didn't have anything to give Mama Gene. All Selah could do was take, and somewhere, maybe not in her spirit, but somewhere real close to it, she wanted to take from Mama Gene.

It hurt Selah, that she would think to hurt her grandmother. She loved Mama Gene. She had bathed Mama Gene. She knew her body and smells in ways that only lovers should know. Selah had sacrificed for her. And though Mama Gene was the reason for Selah being successful, though she was the catalyst for everything good in Selah's life, there are always two sides. And with the loving side down, like the head of a quarter on a flipper's skin, tails had won, and all Selah could feel was hate.

Selah had started bringing crossword puzzles to work on during the times Mama Gene refused to speak to her. Selah looked up from her puzzle and over at the hospital bed. Mama Gene's eyes barely blinked as she concentrated on the horizon of the white wall in front of her. Selah placed her puzzle book down on the small round table and approached the bed. She stared at Mama Gene like she would one of her photography clients. Her skin was thin, like a brown piece of Saran wrap laid loosely over fat and bone. Her pupils had a light blue cataract ring around the edges.

"I'm going with you," Mama Gene said, breaking from her catatonic state. "I'm going with you. I'm going with you."

"You remember me today, Mama Gene?" Selah said, leaning down to her ear.

Mama Gene shook her head yes. "Get my coat. I remember his hands. Mathis had big hands. And they were never cold." She laughed. "Big ole, pancake hands." Mama Gene turned toward the rail and tried to lower it.

"No," Selah said, "you can't get out of bed. We'll go later, Mama Gene. Not right now, okay? We're resting right now. Resting and talking."

"I remember his hands." Mama Gene frowned up her face.

"Yes I know, Mama Gene, Mathis's hands," Selah said in irritation. "Do you remember me, Selah?"

"Ruthie liked Papa." Mama Gene nodded. "Can we go now? - Ruthie's at school. I have to pick her up." Mama Gene's voice got sharp. "I want to go with you."

"I already picked her up for you, Mama Gene; Ruthie is fine."

Selah knew she shouldn't have, she knew she could trigger an episode by asking Mama Gene questions that went too deep. She did it anyway. She just wanted to know if Mama Gene remembered what Selah could never forget.

"Do you remember Michelle, Mama Gene?"

Mama Gene was silent.

Selah got in front of her face to block her view of the wall.

"Mama Gene, do you remember Michelle?"

"Michelle?" she said, after a few moments.

"Yes Mama Gene, my daughter. Do you remember her?"

"Michelle." She played with the name in her mouth. "Michelle. Your daughter?"

Heat burned in Selah's cheeks.

Mama Gene smiled then averted her eyes from Selah to go off inside herself again. Selah sat back down and opened the crossword puzzle book on her lap. She scrolled down the page to find the last question she had answered. Selah hated feeling this way. Her mood - wasn't intentional. It wasn't something she sat in every day to become accustomed to its fit. This feeling was piecemeal, like the placing of true blame.

"Legume," Selah said into the page, as she penciled in another word for bean on the grainy paper.

When Selah looked up, Mama Gene was staring at her.

"You killed that baby," Mama Gene said slowly, a tear forming in her right eye. "I remember."

"And you made me," Selah thought to herself, before she said it aloud.

Chapter Fifty-Six

She went straight to the studio. She just needed to be alone for a while. Regroup. She would have a drink. Maybe she'd even have a pill, one of the pills she'd gotten from Mama Gene's house after the movers had taken all the furniture and all that was left was mismatched Tupperware and pill bottles. Selah had boiled most of the pills and poured the stinking mess down the toilet. A few she kept—as a reminder.

She saved only six. The ones that Mama Gene loved the most. The ones Ruthie Mae would steal from her whenever she happened around. Why couldn't Selah just float away like the rest of the women in her family? That was her God-given right. There was no reason for her not to. All she had to do was commit. Place the tablets on her tongue and wash them down with a hit of scotch.

"Is this what you wanted?"

Her head was ringing. Selah turned around slowly.

Parker sat on the lone stool in her studio with bloodshot eyes.

Selah's Bed

"This is what you wanted, right? What you were always asking me for. For me to pose nude like one of your poster boys."

Selah turned away from Parker and placed the keys on the cabinet.

"Not right now, Parker. I can't. We can talk later."

Selah squatted down and turned the small brass key in the keyhole of the cabinet counterclockwise. She took out a beveled glass bottle of scotch, one shot glass, and sat them both on top of the cabinet.

"Is this what you guys do, drink and have sex right here in my own backyard?"

She tried to keep her voice even, something Parker was normally good at.

"It's not the time for this." She cut him a sharp look.

Parker stood on the partially tarped floor and unbuttoned the last three buttons of his shirt.

"Is this how you do it? Striptease style," he pulled his belt from its loops and let it drop to the floor.

Selah downed the half-filled shot glass. Parker pulled his boxers off with his pants.

"Tell me this, do their dicks get hard when you shoot them?"

Selah sipped another shot. "Parker," she let out an annoyed sigh, "why don't you go pray or something, hunh?" She kept her face to the wall.

"Do you know how embarrassing it is to have a wife like you? *Do you?* You have a gallery with men's dicks on your walls. Don't you disgust yourself?"

"Divorce me." She downed the rest of the shot and absorbed the sting.

"Shoot my picture." He sat nude and hunched over on the stool, gray socks still on his feet. "I want to know what men feel like when they stand nude in front of my wife," Parker paused. "If I didn't believe my soul would burn in hell, I would have divorced you a long time ago. But I stayed. That makes me accountable to you."

"My clients have nothing to do with our problems. I don't—anyway. Put your clothes back on."

"Do you think I'm blind? You think I don't know you screw everything you see? And you still want me to sleep with you at night?"

Selah turned around, looked at Parker, and laughed.

"You don't even curse right. *Screw?* Why don't you just say fuck like the rest of us?"

Selah sat down on the floor with the scotch bottle in her hand.

"Of course you know, Parker, the writing's on the wall, you know what they say, be ye not unequally yoked. Didn't sister what's-her-face tell you that recently, Cathy Jean?" Selah threw the glass stopper at Parker and nicked his leg. "I don't even think you like to *screw.* - That's *your* word, isn't it?"

Parker bent down to throw the stopper back and hit Selah below the kneecap.

"If I'd have known you were a whore, I wouldn't have married you."

"Well if I'da known you'd make me one, I wouldn't have married you either. And I'ma damned good one, so you know." Selah felt a traveling heat spread throughout her chest. She thought back to Mama Gene.

You killed that baby.

"Get out, Parker, I swear. Get out."

She wanted to attack him, she wanted to tear into him like she had Mama Gene. He should have been there for her.

Selah's Bed

You killed that baby looped again in her head.

"I've stood by long enough letting you walk over me. I am your husb—"

"Please," she said indistinguishably into her legs. "I can't take this. Please." Selah got up from the floor and tried to make her way up the stairs.

Parker screamed after her at the bottom step. "I'm not leaving until you do it. Shoot me like you do the rest of your men."

She needed to tune him out and kept walking, despite the lead taking over her legs. The box was sitting on the bed. All she had to do was remember—the feeling didn't start in her throat. It started in her lower lip. If she could just stop the trembling from starting she would be okay.

Selah climbed on the bed and lay there balled into herself. She couldn't stop the tears. This was a guttural cry. The kind of cry that taps into death and sings its song long and hard.

The sound of tears sent a jolt through Parker's chest. He couldn't just leave her there. Something bigger than their argument was going on. Parker ascended the staircase slowly.

Selah scribbled on the back of a baby letter, her eyes blinded from the tears. Parker prayed under his breath as he neared closer to her. He didn't know what to think, but when he sat on the edge of the bed and touched the outside of her arm, his eyes started to fill as well. He took a letter in his hand.

April 26, 1978

I am not good enough to be your mother. I would probably ignore you and not comb your hair every day like mothers are supposed to do. Maybe I would leave you alone like my mother did me. Or maybe the reason I can't have you is because I would beat you. Blame you for every time your father ignores me or tells me he doesn't have time. There has to be some reason like this that I have to give you up. On your last day inside me, I don't know what to say. I don't know how to make things right and say good-bye. There is no good-bye, Michelle. Not for this. All I can do is cry and hope that something happens. I love you, Michelle. I know that you will be with me always. Mama Gene knows, maybe she will change her mind. Maybe he will come. I will call one more time. Then I will pray. I love you. I swear. I love you more than I love myself, but maybe that isn't enough.

"I'm sorry, Selah," he said, hugging his chest to her back.

"You left me, Parker. You left me with a baby and then you left me for God."

"Selah, I didn't know. I was a kid."

"I never sang to her, Parker." Selah sucked in her breath. "I hate you for this. And Mama Gene. And God. She was my baby. *My baby.* If I'd have known you were coming, I would have waited. I wouldn't have—my only baby."

Selah cried and hugged her legs tighter into her chest. Parker placed his face against her hair and let his own tears go. They weren't so different, maybe they were the same. What Parker went to God to make up for, Selah went somewhere else.

Chapter Fifty-Seven

August 23, 2002

It is with sadness that I come to this page today. I am not here to lie and convince myself that what I did has ever been okay. I am not here to blame anyone else and I do not expect you to respect or care that I am crying. But I am crying, Michelle. I have not cried for more than half my life and I have done things that deserve biblical tears. I have done things that have made God cry. My tear ducts have been infected with my denial. I killed you, Michelle. I killed you in my womb for reasons I thought were strong enough to take another's life. I thought you were going to take mine. I thought that with you I would have been destined to relive the lives of my mother and my grandmother. I thought you would bury me under the smell of your bottled milk and diaper changes. I convinced myself of this, and I missed you every moment afterward.

I saw so many in my neighborhood buried alive. Waterman Gardens was the tombstone that every day announced where I was going. I do not expect you to understand, I do not expect you to forgive. I have lived with your ghosts. They are in my toothpaste in the morning and in the lining of my socks. I have walked with your ghosts and sexed near strangers in their presence. They do not go away.

I am coming to you, not knowing how to make up for something I cannot change. I have imagined a life for you. You were loved in this life. You were mine in this life. I heard the timbre in your cry and you sucked hard stubborn milk from my breasts. You loved me back in this life, Michelle. You slept in bed with me at night and you held my face and pinched my cheeks to fall asleep. I convinced myself of these things. Your hair is a reddish brown because you take after your father when he was little. You have his thick eyebrows and my coarse hair. I know everything about you, Michelle, even what you smell like when you are sick.

You are my daughter. I made you in my body. I felt you plant your life into the left wall of my pelvic lining. You grew. And every new sign of your presence scared me. I wanted blood more than I wanted you. I wanted my life back before it was taken. That's why I listened to Mama Gene. Then he didn't call me. He made me choose alone. Like I had climbed inside my womb and fucked myself. He was not my first, but he was my only possibility. He was not my first, but I loved him. I would not make him stay because of you. I would not make him choose me so that I could be second to a different kind of dream he would think about while breathing hate on my sleeping neck as he hugged me at night. I would not be the ghetto girl who climbed out of the ghetto on man's dick. But I hated him for this, more than I have ever loved anyone. I hated him for not standing up for me or us or you. I hated him for not knowing and not calling and not coming and making me choose by myself. There is no one else to blame for my sin. There is no higher counsel to look to or question. Even God was silent.

Parker tells me that I have to let go of you now, the same way he has to. I do not feel capable of this. I have shown him all of the letters and the picture

Selah's Bed

I took of my stomach when I was one month pregnant with you. I want to let you know that you were my last child. I would have done anything to dig your body from the chemical waste bag in the doctor's office. I would have uncrushed your bones and reshaped your head after they sucked and scraped you out of my tilted pelvis if I could have. You were small but looming large and I did not know how important you were until you were over. I asked for your placenta. I cried for your placenta and they would not give it to me. I wanted to carry a piece of you home in my purse.

You would have been a girl. I didn't ask them because I couldn't afford to know in that moment of blood and cold metal. And though I am sorry beyond the ability to ask forgiveness, and though you never had one breath, I am saddest for myself. That I never heard you laugh. That I never held your warm foot to my face and played stinky feet. That I never sang you nursery rhymes. I never sang to you, Michelle. Hush, hush, hush little baby. Hush. Momma is trying to sleep. Hush. If I had sung to you, maybe you would be here right now. I would not let myself sing to you, not even in my womb. Please hush.

You cry. You sit behind my heart and cry until the aching starts in my throat and I bowl over. For twenty-one years you have cried. I have talked to women about this. Even Tina Perkins and Tasha-Marie from my old neighborhood. They did not know back then when I dropped out of school and hid myself in pea green walls and shriveled to your crying. They do not know about you still, but they have told me about their ghosts.

They say that all dead children live. They live in the little things. Coffee cups and socks like you do. Tasha-Marie always heard a ringing in her ears and she just built her other children on top of it. Tina said that her two aborted children were the reason for her three miscarriages because they were still angry and wouldn't let her move on until she acknowledged them.

I am acknowledging you. I am acknowledging you. I am acknowledging you. And I will not ask you to forgive me.

Chapter Fifty-Eight

They burned the letters in a white porcelain bowl, much like the one Peter had used to pour vegetarian chili in the first time Selah ever saw him. There were fifteen letters on letterhead and thirty scribbled notes written on various sizes of scratch paper.

"Are you ready?" Parker asked.

Selah nodded and bit into her lip to stop the tremble.

Parker rolled up a twig of the Sunday newspaper and placed it in the blue-red flame on the stove. He handed it to Selah.

She took a deep breath and extended the fire into the bowl. They watched as the pages turned to ash.

Selah and Parker buried them together. In the backyard, next to the fence. Parker carried the shovel from the garage; Selah carried the ashes in the same box she had kept the letters in for all those years. They placed a stone plaque on the fresh mound of dirt and prayed. Selah was ready to ask for forgiveness now. Parker was ready to stop trying to buy it from God. Nothing was fixed, but two people who had lost each other years ago had found a thread. And like anything that is broken but still alive, they would try to put themselves back together again.

In loving memory,

Michelle Wells Lareaux

oooo

Acknowledgments

This book is especially for my mother and father: Bertha and Virgil.
When I was a teenager, my father was stabbed seven times one evening
and spent that Father's Day in the critical care unit at Loma Linda University Hospital. I took his Father's Day gift of a triple decker tackle
box and fishing paraphernalia to the hospital that year. He made it out.

This past year, the day before I was leaving to do a signing at the
Essence Music Festival after the publication of my first book, my
mother was hospitalized at Loma Linda University Hospital from a
heart attack and Adult Respiratory Distress Syndrome. My mother was
given a six percent chance to live. She made it out.

I surrender this story to them out of their courage and fighting
spirit. I am forever grateful that I have my beautiful parents with me
today and I am truly grateful for every step along our collective path.

I am thankful to my husband, Michael, for being the beautiful man
and light that he is, my brother/friend Edgar, my sister Lossie, my sister
Jolena, my friend Nancy Padron, my dad, and everyone else whom I

Acknowledgments

may not be thinking of in this specific moment who was on the frontline in the past year of my life as I was being a mother to my own mother. This book may not have been possible without your support because I was living pieces of this story as I was writing it.

Thank you so very much to my beautiful editor, Dominick Anfuso, and my agent, Jim Levine, for bearing with me in this process. I love you guys. Kristen McGuiness, I am glad to call you a friend. Martha Levin, Carisa Hays, Suzanne Donahue, Amy Heller, Wylie O'Sullivan, and Isolde Sauer, and everyone at the Free Press, you are top-notch and I am so honored to work with you.

To the crew: my family, my friends, The World Stage, PEN Center USA West, UCLA Extension Writing Program, My Hamlet and Silence Family, to everyone I interviewed and to the residence I know and love in San Bernardino: Monsha, Billy, Nicole, Michael, Crystal, Zuana, Robert, Lydia, Fred, Virgil Jr., Morris, Michelle, Zettie, Yoggie, Jamal, Rashaun, Kaylawni, Kayshawn, Dae'zha, Tut, LaVonne, Virginia, Jay, Sarah, Ambria, Anthony, Candice, Dee Black, AK Toney, Paul Calderon, Liz, Lakimba, Jessica, Cherise Alley, Xiomara Gumbs, Gladys Steen, Alex Datcher, Dr. Linda Venis, Rick Noguchi, Lady Walquer, Delane Vaughn, Miss Ruth, Kimberly Branch, Jan Ebey, Mr. Serrao, Mr. Metternick, Ms. Anderson, Mrs. Rowe, Mrs. Agnolia Davis, Robert Cole Sr., Mary Wade, Mary Louise, Terry, Joe Hunter, Dogan Wilson, Avie Wilson, Daphne Adams, Richard May, the Brown Family, Shelley and Norvel McDonald, Janet Fitch, Jervy Tervalon, Colin Channer (thank you for the kick-ass compliment: my writing is like fine cuisine . . . making me crack a smile), Marie Brown (you are absolutely inspiring), Miss Terry (thank you for the time and direction—even if I am hard-headed), the critical care staff at Loma Linda University Hospital, Joan, Melissa, Melynda, Miek, and all of JLC—thank you.

Thank you to EsoWon, Maliks, Phenix, Hueman, Medu, African

Acknowledgments

Spectrum, and to all the beautiful bookstore owners and staff who have been *soooo* supportive.

Over the last two years I have met some of the most amazing women (and a few men) from book clubs around the country. Because I *know* I will forget someone, I would just like to say thank you for the gatherings, food, camaraderie, heated discussions, online chats, city tours, tears, T-shirts, and love.

To everyone living through Alzheimer's disease, elderly adult care, prescription-drug addiction—directly or indirectly—keep getting back up.

Thank you God for sustaining me with joy and peace. Selah.

About the Author

Jenoyne Adams is the author of the bestselling novel *Resurrecting Mingus*. She is a poet, journalist, PEN Center USA West Emerging Voices fellow, and member of the World Stage Anansi Writer's Workshop in Leimert Park. She has been featured in programs at the National Black Arts Festival, the Schomburg Museum, the Essence Music Festival, and the J. Paul Getty Museum. Her poetry and prose have been featured in *Brown Sugar II, Catch the Fire: A Cross-Generational Anthology of Contemporary African-American Poetry,* and *Black Expressions: The Best Erotic Writings from Individuals of African-American Descent.* She was born in San Bernardino, California, and lives in Los Angeles with her husband, writer Michael Datcher.

A Conversation with Jenoyne Adams

Selah's Bed is a beautiful, haunting novel of self-discovery and redemption. Just before its publication in paperback, Jenoyne Adams took some time to talk to her Free Press editor about how she came to write the book and create its memorable characters.

Q: How long did it take you to write *Selah's Bed*?

A: I wrote *Selah's Bed* over a period of two years, though during the same period I was the primary caregiver for my mother, who was ill at the time. It was a very different experience from that of writing *Resurrecting Mingus,* but I value it immensely because I grew a lot in the process.

Q: Did you know how the book was going to end when you started writing, or did the plot unfold as you went?

A: I think the plot always unfolds as you go, though you start out thinking that you know everything that's going to happen during the course of writing. It's almost like magic. You plan and put everything in its perfect place, then as you write and keep getting to know your characters, you find out that some of what you thought would happen is plausible and that other things need to be saved for a different book.

Q: Though smart, beautiful, talented, and, ultimately, caring, Selah is a very troubled, and troubling, character. Did you ever find it hard spending so much time with her, as it were?

A: No, I never found it hard to spend time with Selah. I think it is a powerful journey to really know someone. Most of us, with most people, operate on surface levels. We know what is wonderful, nice, and good about the people in our lives. These acceptable qualities are the things we like to put in front of our scars. It seems like much more of a fantastic journey to know someone deeply, becoming aware of flaws and shortcomings as well as all of the good stuff. Now, don't get me wrong, I wouldn't want Selah around my husband *(smile)*, but I feel truly honored to have been exposed to someone's inner workings the way I was exposed to Selah's.

Q: It's only recently that many writers and other artists have begun to acknowledge that extramarital affairs and psychological unavailability are not solely male territory, and it is still much more common for a female character to be cast in the role of emotionally giving caretaker, or emotionally needy victim. Did you have real or fictional models in mind when you made Selah the unavailable one in the marriage, or did you invent her entirely?

A: I think more than anything, Selah's pain shaped who she became. So for me, being aware of her pain more than anything else, I needed to figure out what had happened in her life to make her do the things that she did. Her sexual appetite was a product of her experience. I don't recall thinking of anyone in particular when I wrote about her, but we all know people like Selah, whether we realize it or not. People who mask their hurts with food, alcohol, sex, exercise, religion—so much so that they may not even remember the events that brought them to their current circumstance. Selah does remember. Her problem is that sex is the only thing that helps her to pretend a little.

Q: What about Mama Gene? She is such a wonderful and complicated mix of matron and curmudgeon. Is she modeled on anyone in particular?

A: I think much like Selah, Mama Gene has learned how to survive in her environment. People often underestimate the effects "hard living" can have on the body, not to mention the soul. Mama Gene has experienced soul wounds and some of her tough attitudes toward Selah are to save Selah from a similar fate. Some of her harmful behaviors toward herself are to medicate the pain. Have you ever had a parent tell you never to fall asleep with the television on, but they do it all the time themselves? Selah and Mama Gene's relationship is kind of like this. So yes, again, I have seen people throughout life with similar behaviors, but rather than modeling my characters after anyone specifically, I rather help the characters create their own realities.

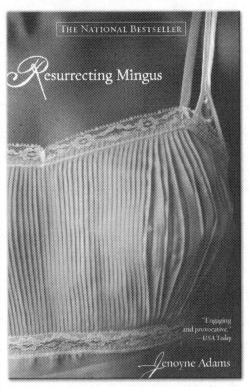

Printed in the United States
By Bookmasters